CARDINAL

K. KELLY

Cardinal
The Affinity Chronicles Book One

K. Kelly

Disclaimer: The material in this book contains graphic language and sexual content and is intended for mature audiences, ages 18 and older.

ISBN: 978-1-922883-12-4

Editing by Swish Design & Editing
Proofreading by Swish Design & Editing
Book design by Swish Design & Editing
Cover design by Christian Bentulan at Covers by Christian
Cover Image Copyright 2020
First Edition 2020
Kathleen Kelly writing as K. Kelly
Copyright © 2020 K. Kelly
All Rights Reserved

DEDICATION

I love things that go bump in the night in books.
I'm not good with things that go bump in the night
in real life, and that's when my hubby, SL,
saves me.
For all the times you've assured me it's just a cat, a
possum, or pretended to catch that spider or bug
and disposed of it outside because I won't let you
kill it.

Thank you.

So, my dear readers, this one is for the one I love
the most.

CARDINAL

PROLOGUE

The world has been divided into races, and all are aware except for the humans. If they can find the chosen one, the one who will unite all the races, then and only then will the humans become aware of us.

Occasionally, some of the gifted or the half-breed humans see us, but for the most part, we are the things of myth and legend.

There are eight races.

Choir – Angels
Clutch - Vampires
Coven – Witches Herd
– Faeries

Tribe – Humans

Troupe - Elves

The battle is on to find the chosen one. All we know for certain is that she's female. As for her race, no one knows. Many believe she'll be of the tribe, but each race hopes she'll come from their line. For whoever she is, she will wield great power over all.

Each of the races wishes to have control over such power and rule the earth.

CHAPTER ONE

Janardan – The World's Oldest Vampire

The night is ending. After a thousand years of roaming the earth, I can feel it in my bones—that slight prickle as daylight begins its emergence into the world. I haven't fed. Casting a look around the room, all I can see are drunkards, junkies, or other supernaturals. The demon, Baracus, tilts his head in my direction, and out of habit, I bare my fangs at him. The long-dead feud is not forgotten by either of us. We both lost many during the wars. Slowly, neck exposed, he approaches me.

"What?" I ask in a bored tone.

"You look good, Janardan, but I fear you've left your run too late. The humans who are here are neither evil-doers nor worthy of you."

"You presume to know who's worthy of me?"

"I meant no offense, only stating a fact."

Baracus is right. For the better part of four hundred years, I've only fed off the underbelly of society—those whose blood is tainted. It's what's kept me alive. If I'd allowed myself the innocents, they would have ended me centuries ago. I am the oldest of my kind. I could feed on Baracus, but demon blood tastes awful, and although I could survive on it, I'd prefer not to.

"Why are you here?"

"The Council has demanded an audience of all the races. Isn't that why you're here in New York City?"

I shake my head slightly, and the demon lets his mask slip for a moment, and I see the thing underneath. Baracus' flesh hangs off in places, and his tusks nearly reach his cheekbones. Picture a wild boar, only worse.

"You're showing your true face to me, why?"

"We both lost many in the war. I have no desire to revisit old wounds. The Council should have invited you since you're the oldest."

"The oldest but not in charge, that goes to Levi. I have no desire to usher in the newest generation. They make so many mistakes."

"Times are changing. The witches believe she's among us. The one who can unite all the races and bring peace."

I huff at him and shake my head. Every few decades, the witches believe the great one is among us. And every few decades, they are wrong. It makes sense I wasn't invited. The last time I was summoned was one hundred years ago. I killed the head of the witches' coven and had to go into hiding. They cursed me by way of a ring that as I look at it, it begins to glow. "Fuck," I mutter.

"The witches?"

I sigh and scowl. "Yes, the witches."

"I know where the meeting is. I could take you?"

The ring begins to burn my skin, and I don't feel well. "Take me to them. Lead the way."

Baracus nods, but I know having a predator at your back isn't a comfortable feeling. Every so often, he glances over his shoulder at me, and time and again, he rubs the back of his neck.

Baracus leads me through the seedy side of New York City, many of his kind hide here. As we pass the fifth demon, I match Baracus' pace and walk beside him.

"If you try to kill me or one of your kind does, I promise to take you with me," I state as I stare straight ahead.

"Not tonight, Liberator. I have no desire for a witches' ring. Those things are certain death."

Liberator, an old name that I haven't heard in a long time. I twist the ring around my finger, the burning sensation increases as does the sickness. It overwhelms me, and I lean up against the brick wall of the alley we are in. "How much further?"

"You don't look good."

"How much further," I repeat in a stronger tone.

"Another ten minutes or so. There's a secret door at the end of this alley."

I nod at him and push-off, then stumble, and the demon reaches out to steady me. My fangs extend, and I growl in his fake face—the face he projects to the humans—but I know what he is.

"Janardan, you have to trust me. The witches are summoning you, it's why the ring has been activated. I can help you if you'll let me." "Why?"

I ground out.

"There are those of us who believe you're the key."

I huff at him and bark out a laugh. "Demon, have you lost your mind? If I were the key, I'd have solved this a long time ago. Instead, my kind is relegated to the darkness, never seeing the light. If I could solve that age-old problem, I would."

"You believe that when the races are united, your kind will be able to walk in the light?"

"Yes."

Baracus' eyes widen. "It would mean the end of the humans."

"No, I don't believe it would. There would be rules in place much like there are now."

I look up at the sky and can see the first flickers of sunlight shoot across. If I don't get undercover soon, I'll be in worse shape than I am right now.

"We need to hurry, Baracus. Daylight is here."

Baracus follows my gaze, nods, and takes off for the end of the alley at a faster pace. For us, it's a slow jog, but for the humans, we would be beyond their comprehension and appear to them as wind. A blur.

Baracus opens a door, turns left, and opens a trap door, motioning for me to drop down into it.

"If this is a trap, I promise to end you slowly."

Baracus lets his mask fall away, so I'm left looking into his true face. "I give you my word."

"Such as it is for a demon."

I smile at him and jump into the hole, finding myself falling. After ten seconds, I realize I'm in a witches' trap. I feel like I'm falling, but in truth, I am in one spot. Frozen in time until the witches decide what to do with me. In frustration, I roar into the abyss.

My name is Janardan, liberator from the cycle of birth and death, and I will not be held captive by anyone.

CHAPTER TWO

Evie: High Witch

"Well done, Baracus. You brought him to us."

"He'll gut me for this. You must let him go. Janardan will not stand for this type of insult."

I look over at the demon, his true face is on display. "Pull yourself together. Janardan will not be hurt. We only wish to read his aura, and the pit is the easiest way to do it. Vampires often take on the aura of their last meal. This way we'll see his true colors."

The demon slips his projected face back on. It's much better than his real face, handsome even. Baracus purses his lips and shifts from side to side. A small frown furrows his brow.

"Janardan isn't any vampire. He's the oldest, and

if he wanted to, he could lead the clutch. They wouldn't be able to say no to him. Evie, *please* let him go."

I look at him with distaste. Baracus isn't telling me something I don't already know. And I also know as the one who led Janardan to us, he'll be the first that he goes hunting for. I can't help it. I smile.

"Relax, this will only take a few minutes. He's not being harmed, and the spell on the ring is being wound down at the same time. Janardan will be better than he was before."

"You have to explain to him why you're doing this!"

I scoff at him. "I don't answer to *you*."

I look back at Janardan as he hangs in mid-air, fangs extended, coat and long brown hair flying upward. He's no longer thrashing about, his eyes are closed, and I'm guessing he's using his senses to try and decipher how many of us are around him. Janardan turns his body, opens his eyes, and stares directly at me. Impressive.

I flick a glance at Baracus whose human face has lost all color.

"Be calm, Baracus. He can't see us. He's probably zoomed in on my heat signature. Vampires are predictable predators."

Without looking at me, Baracus speaks. "If you think there's anything predictable about him, you're insane. Janardan survived the wars, survived the plagues, and he's unstoppable."

"You survived the wars, too, so it doesn't count for much."

Janardan laughs as though he's heard our conversation, but I know that's not possible. I turn around and walk from the room. The hairs on the back of my neck stand up. I open the door to the other chamber where our most powerful witches are gathered.

"Well? What's his aura?"

After the wars, aura colors became harder to identify. And they don't always mean what they used to. Right now, Baracus' aura is white, which used to mean pure. This demon is anything but pure.

Abigail, the oldest of us, clucks her tongue. "You're not going to believe it."

I sigh and arch an eyebrow at her.

"Cardinal red."

I gasp and move to the window to see Janardan better.

"Not possible! Could this be a mistake? Are you reading him properly?"

Cardinal

Abigail comes to stand beside me, her long gray hair brushes against my arm.

"Open yourself up, Evie. You'll see it, too."

I take in a deep breath, let it out slowly, and open my mind. When I can feel Baracus and the other three witches in the room, I center myself and open my eyes. True enough, the vampire is surrounded in a deep red—cardinal red.

"How can this be?"

Gloria places a hand on my shoulder. "He's linked to her."

"No! Janardan has not been included in any Council business. He's not even the head of his clutch. There is no way," I state.

Patricia moves to stand next to Abigail. "You see the proof for yourself."

I close off my mind, and Janardan's aura fades away. "Do you think he knows where she is?" I ask them.

Abigail shakes her head. "No. You're right, Janardan knows nothing of the Council's dealings. For over one hundred years, he's kept to himself, only dealing with us if he has to. The last time he was called, he killed the head of our order, and that little trinket on his finger keeps him in line. We'd know if he'd found her, she's the only one who can free him."

Kathleen Kelly

Baracus inhales, and we turn to him.

"Poor demon, you've heard way too much," I say as he backs away from us.

"Do we kill him?" asks Gloria with a grin.

"No, we can't kill him. He's the head of his legion, pitiful as he is. Abigail, can you take this day from him?"

The old witch purses her lips and squints at the demon. "Yes, but it will take two of us to purge the day from him. He'll have no recollection of meeting Janardan or us. Demons are the easiest to manipulate. Although there is a problem. He associates with the angel, Tristan, and if Tristan suspects Baracus has been hexed, he can undo it and release the memory."

"It'd be easier to kill him," suggests Gloria.

"As much as I'd like to, we can't. The legion would come looking for us, and their numbers are large." I look at Abigail and Patricia. "Do it! Take the day and pray that the angel, Tristan, suspects nothing."

CHAPTER THREE

Angelica Adam

Have you ever noticed how the subway at night is always filled with large hulking men who could break you in half at any moment? But through the day, it's all business suits and normality. Well, except for the creeper who insists on sitting in the same car as me. It's like he waits for me. I've nicknamed him Sam the Stalker. Right now, I'd be happy to have Sam on the platform. I glance up at the group of men at the far end. They're getting louder, and their rough-housing is becoming more violent. I move further away and position myself behind a tiled pole, hoping they won't notice me.

"You shouldn't be down here alone."

I yelp in surprise and discover a tall man standing next to me. His skin is tanned, and his eyes are bright green, perfectly framed with blond eyebrows. He's not looking at me though, he's looking at the men. I follow his gaze, and they're all looking at us.

"Oh, shit," I whisper.

"You should leave."

The men point at us, and one moves toward us.

"Mister, I think we should both leave."

"I don't run from legion."

"Oh, you know them? Is that one called Legion?"

With a smile on his lips, he shakes his head and places two fingers on the middle of my forehead.

"Angelica?"

I move away from his touch.

"How do you know my name?"

He's not looking at me but behind me. "Run!" he yells.

I cast a look over my shoulder, and the men all seem to have masks on. They look like big, scary trolls.

A scream escapes me, and I run for the subway stairs. Glancing over my shoulder, I look at the man, and he seems taller somehow, and he's holding a staff.

"Angelica, run, seek the light and the herd," roars the man.

I don't need to be told twice. I run as fast as my legs can carry me up the stairs, but when I get to the top, there is no light, only darkness. There must be a blackout.

Running blindly down the street, I'm looking for someone, anyone to protect me. Up ahead, I see a grocery store open, and a man is out the front with a torch. I head for the light and hopefully, safety.

"Help," I yell as I stumble and trip right into his arms. When I look up at him, he looks remarkably like the man in the subway.

"Whoa! What's wrong?"

"There's a gang in the subway and a man, and he told me to run."

The man laughs, and I notice he's getting taller, thinner, and is starting to glow.

I let go of him and move back. "What are you?" I ask.

The man looks down at himself and frowns. "How did you do that, little human?"

"Do what?"

"See my true form."

This night just went from boringly normal to completely fucked up in no time flat.

"Your true form? Mister, there's a guy in the subway about to get his ass kicked by a gang. He told me to seek the light and the herd." *Someone must have spiked my drink, that is if I'd been drinking.* "I need to go." I look further down the street, but it's all in darkness.

The shopkeeper reaches out and touches me on the forehead, much the same as the man before him.

"Oh, dear," he exclaims.

I flinch away from him and rub my forehead. I open my mouth to speak, and he holds up a finger. "Hear me, little one, the herd can't protect you. The legion has your scent now. Run. And pray another race will serve you better. My brother should not have intervened. Look for the signs, for they will be all around you. Run!"

I back up, take a few steps to the side, and run down the street away from him. The darkness feels like it's closing in on me, and I'm sure there are evil things lurking all around. I pump my legs, scared beyond words, only concentrating on getting as far away from the subway as possible. Suddenly, I'm in the middle of Times Square, light, lots of it, and people surround me.

How the hell did I get here?

A hand clasps my shoulder, and I'm spun around. Standing in front of me is a policeman. I grasp his hand in mine, and just like before, he morphs into something else. Only this time it's an angel, complete with wings and a halo.

"I've been drugged!"

He looks down and frowns. "Ma'am, I need you to calm down."

"What are you?"

"What are you?" the policeman loud whispers as he leans into me.

"My name is Angelica Adam." I walk around him, touching his wings as I circle him. "Are you an angel? Am I dead?"

Laughter erupts from a policeman not three feet away. "Well, that's a new one! Tristan, she thinks you're an angel." The policeman flutters his hands and bats his eyelids.

"Put a lid on it, Murphy! Clearly, she's on something." The angel grabs me by the elbow and leads me further away from his partner. "Whatever you are, stop it. If you project too much, everyone will see me, and that's bad."

"That's bad? Not everyone can see you?"

With an exasperated sigh, he touches me on the forehead, but this time I pass out.

Darkness claims me.

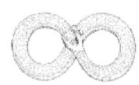

There's an annoying beeping sound which is pulling me from my slumber. I'm warm and cozy and don't want to wake just yet. Someone grabs my wrist, and I open my eyes.

"Ahh, you're awake. Do you know where you are?" asks a woman in blue scrubs.

"The hospital?"

"Good. What's your name?"

"Angelica Adam. How did I end up here?"

The nurse smiles at me. "The policeman who brought you in seemed to think you'd been drugged. We didn't find anything in your system, your tox screen was clean. How are you feeling?"

"Good, fine. How long have I been here?"

She picks up my chart and scans it. "Four hours. Think you can stand?"

I nod, and she helps me to get out of the bed. When my feet hit the floor, I look down at my hospital gown and frown. "Where are my clothes?"

The nurse chuckles. "In the cupboard behind me along with your purse. I'm going to get a doctor to discharge you. While I do that, how about you get dressed?"

I nod, and as soon as she's out of the room, I frantically put my clothes on. I'm pulling on my shoes when the policeman pokes his head through the door.

"How are you feeling, Angelica?"

"What did you do to me?" I demand to know.

He comes further into the room, making sure the door is closed. "How are you feeling?" he asks again, his eyes glowing weirdly.

"I'm fine. I feel..." Truthfully, I feel fantastic. The way I've felt after a good meal and some sleep, only better, more energized. "I feel great."

He smiles at me and tilts his head to the side. "What are you?"

"What do you mean?"

"What race are you?"

"I'm human, like you."

The policeman walks toward me and grabs my hand. He inhales then says, "Truth."

As I stare at him, he glows brighter, and I can see wings and a halo.

Gasping, I pull out of his grasp. "You're an angel?"

He looks down, frowns, and looks up at me. "Angelica Adam, are you a witch?"

"I beg your pardon? A witch?"

He chuckles, and the noise is music to my ears.

"I'm the archangel, Tristan, and you're no ordinary human. Perhaps you are a half-breed?"

I rub my eyes and slowly open them. Unfortunately, he still looks like an angel.

"The nurse said there was nothing on my tox screen, but surely that must be wrong? I just heard you say that you're the archangel, Tristan, and I can see wings, a halo, and you're glowing."

"You're glowing, too."

I turn around and stare at my reflection in the mirror stuck on the back of the bathroom door, and sure enough, a dark red light is all around me.

"What does that mean?"

"How old are you, Angelica?"

"Today is my twenty-fifth birthday."

"For she'll come into her power in her twentyfifth year, and when she touches the dutiful, their true selves will become known to her. She will be all-powerful and guide us to redemption."

I frown at him. "Tristan, what was that?"

"A verse from a very old book. I was beginning to believe you didn't exist yet, here you are."

"I don't know who or what you think I am, but Tristan, I need to get home. I need to sleep this off, whatever it is. Hell, I'm probably standing here talking to myself. This can't be real." I close my eyes and slap each side of my face hard. When I open them, Tristan is still standing in front of me, grinning at me like he's won the lottery.

"What?"

"We need to get you out of here. Do you have somewhere safe to go?"

"Tristan, I want to go home. It's been a weird day."

As though I'm unable to stop myself, I reach out and touch his wing. The feathers are so soft, and a feeling of happiness invades my being. I sigh and look into Tristan's eyes, and he's grinning down at me. His wings move and encircle me, pulling me closer to him. I'm pushed up against his welldefined chest.

"Umm, Tristan?"

"Close your eyes and think of home."

"Tristan..."

"Shhh, Angelica, concentrate." I feel his chest expand, and he slowly lets out a breath. "May I enter your abode?"

"We're in the hospital."

Tristan chuckles, and I feel warm and loved. "A simple yes or no, please."

"Sure, yes, please come in," I say as I giggle.

I take a deep breath, and he smells so good like freshly baked cookies or your favorite candy. The scent is overwhelming, but I can't seem to breathe enough of him in. When I open my eyes, I'm standing in the middle of my apartment. Alone. My cat, Grace, is staring up at me. She walks toward me, hisses, and stops mid-step.

"What is it, fat girl?" I ask her. Grace shakes her head, then continues toward me. "Do you know how I got here?" Grace meows and walks to her food dish. "Right, you don't care." I chuckle. "I think someone drugged me."

I look around my apartment, but I'm the only one here. When I check the front door it's bolted from the inside, my keys are on the hook, and my handbag is in its usual spot.

Did I imagine the last few hours?

I look at the clock on the wall in the kitchen, and it says two in the morning.

I left work at six, and now it's two.

None of this makes any sense.

So I feed my cat and crawl into bed, fully clothed. I know it's strange, but my clothes smell so good.

CHAPTER FOUR

Angelica Adam

"Trust me," says the voice in my dreams.

I shake my head. There's something he's not telling me.

"Give me your body," the voice whispers.

I can feel hands blazing a trail from my nipples to my most sensitive region. When he touches me there, I part my legs and let him ignite the passion that threatens to overwhelm me. My body is on fire, and all I can think about is the pleasure of this man's touch.

"Give me your body," he repeats as he sucks on my nipple.

Heat is building within me, and I want nothing more than for him to take me over the edge. His mouth makes its way further down my frame, his kisses are divine, and when he gets to my pussy and licks me, I think I'm going to explode. His tongue plunges into me, and he sucks my clit. The feeling is amazing. His fingers dig into my hips, and I rock them to give him better access.

"Say I can have you," whispers the voice. "Tell me I can have your body."

"Yes," I cry, desperate for release.

"Yes?"

"Yes!" My fingers entwine in his hair and hold him there as he licks, sucks, and probes me as the pressure within me builds.

"Say the words, Angelica. Say I can have your body."

With release being my only thought, I nod.

"The words."

This time he sounds angry, and I don't want to disappoint him, but a small part of me wonders why? Why do I have to say the words? And there's a noise, someone else is here. His mouth is back on me as he sucks, licks and his tongue plunges inside me. I'm so close.

"Tell me what I need to hear," he whispers.

Then he sucks on my clit, and I'm done for, the orgasm washes through me, and I ride his face, holding him in place until I'm well spent. The aftershocks keep coming, and he sucks and licks, drinking me in.

"Let me have you," he whispers.

I try to open my eyes, but I can't. I feel his shoulders, and they are strong, hard, and there's something else but it's soft. I reach further down, and he's covered in softness. Finally, my eyes open, and I'm alone in my bed with the radio on, completely naked and covered in sweat. "Ange!" Bang.

Bang.

Bang.

"Ange! Are you home?"

I sit bolt upright and look at my phone. It's one o'clock in the afternoon. I've slept half the day away.

"Ange!"

I scramble out of bed, put on a robe, and run to my front door. I throw it open and standing there is my best friend and work colleague, Chris.

"Jesus!" yells Chris. "I was worried about you. Why didn't you answer your phone or come into work today? Or call? Or?" Then dramatically, he waves his arms in distress.

I take a step out into the hallway, and he pulls me into a bone-crushing hug.

"Chris?" I gasp.

"Why do you have sex hair? Have you stayed home all day to have sex?" Then he whispers, "Is he still here?"

I pull back from him, shaking my head. "No. I had a weird night, and I guess I overslept."

"I've called you a hundred times. Drew wasn't at all happy you didn't come in today, but it's cool, I covered for you. I told him you were sick. Okay?"

My face softens. Chris is my only friend. We met the first day I started at the magazine. He showed me the ropes and guided me to the best cheapest coffee in the city. Without Chris, I wouldn't have anyone.

"Let's go inside. I'll make us both a drink."

"Why do you smell so good, like... cookies or..." Chris pulls back and looks me in the eyes. "Oh no! Did you say yes?"

"Yes?"

"Did you give the angel permission?"

I take two steps back from Chris. "What do you mean?"

Chris hits himself on the side of his head and balls his hands into fists. "Fuck! Yesterday was your birthday, wasn't it? You're twenty-five!"

"Yes..."

Chris looks at me, a scowl on his handsome face. "I'm going to be in so much trouble. Why didn't you mention it was your birthday yesterday?"

"Why do you think I took *twenty-five* cupcakes to work? And why are *you* in trouble?"

"Shit! I didn't notice there were twenty-five. Did you fuck the angel?"

I back further into my apartment, hand on the door frame ready to slam it closed. Chris' features soften, and he sighs. Slowly, he unballs his fists and tries to smile. His face now looks incredibly sad.

"Chris, what's going on?" I whisper.

"Angelica, please let me come in and explain. I was assigned to you. I had one job. Dammit! Just one job." Chris holds up a finger, waving it in the air.

"You're my best friend. For a human, you've been a lot of fun."

For a human, you've been a lot of fun?

What the hell does that mean?

"I don't understand," I reply, shaking my head.

Chris drops down onto one knee with his eyes downcast. "On my life and the blood of my clan, I promise, I'll never hurt you. Please, Ange, let me in." I move to one side and gesture for him to enter. "You need to invite me in," he states.

"Are you a vampire?"

Chris chuckles. "No. But now you've come into your own, I'll need an invite every time I try to enter your house. The other races *should* be the same."

"Please, come in, Chris."

He stands and moves past me so quickly all I feel is the wind as he rushes past. I shut the door and find him sitting at my dining room table, looking nervous.

"H-How did you do that?"

"I'm going to start from the beginning. I'm an elf. My real name is Eruaphadion... air-oo-ah-fahd-eeon. In English, it translates to Christopher. I was assigned to you by the troupe, my clan, to protect and guide you through your transition."

"My transition?"

"Would you like me to make you a coffee or tea?"

"Chris, what the fuck is going on?"

"I'm going to make tea. You smell like angel. Go shower. I promise to answer all of your questions. Remember, Angelica, *I am* your friend."

I look at him skeptically. I have no reason to distrust him, but he sounds completely bonkers. Chris stands, and I hold out my hand to him. He tilts his head to the side and then places his hand in mine. The person before me blurs, and I blink a few times as he gradually becomes taller, thinner, and his short dark hair morphs and becomes long dark hair. His ears lengthen and become pointy, his skin glows, and Chris has gone from a very ordinarylooking young man to someone so beautiful it's almost hard to look him in the eyes.

"Oh my God!" I let go of him and stumble back a few paces.

"Ange, it's okay. It's me, Chris."

"No! Whatever you are, you're *not* Chris."

"We have coffee every day at lunchtime at a food cart one hundred feet from where we work. I held your hair back at the staff Christmas party when you drank too much. We make fun of Drew, our boss, whenever he turns his back. I know your favorite color is light pink, so light it's almost white. Your favorite scent is roses and that you save to buy it as you like to wear the one from that expensive boutique in Paris, and they make only one hundred and fifty bottles a year. I know—"

"Stop!"

"Ange—"

"No!"

Chris shuffles from foot to foot, and now that he's in elf form, he makes it look graceful. How does he do that? I'm chewing on my bottom lip, and I can see he wants to speak but is doing as I ask.

"I need to shower." Chris nods. "I can't trust you in my apartment."

"If I were going to hurt you, I'd have done so before now. I belong to the troupe, but you now command me."

"What does that mean?"

"I'll obey any command you give me."

"How do I know you're not lying? You've lied to me for two years. And all these weird things are happening. Why didn't you tell me?"

Chris holds up his hands and nods. The movement is graceful, and there's an air of regality about him. "I was forbidden to. We came across you by accident—"

"Stop! Just stop." I slump down in a chair, all my energy from before feels like it's seeping out of me.

Chris kneels in front of me and places two fingers on the middle of my forehead. "Oh, no! How are you feeling?"

"I'm suddenly exhausted." My eyelids feel very heavy.

"Angelica... I need you to stay awake. Do you understand?"

I nod, but his voice is becoming so soft. I try to focus on his mouth, and I can see his lips moving, but I have no idea what he's saying. I shake my head a couple of times trying to clear the fog that's invaded my mind.

Chris leans down and picks me up. He carries me into the bathroom and puts me in the shower, turning on the cold water. I can feel it, and I know I should be shivering, and maybe I am, but sleep wants to claim me.

"No. *No.* NO!" chants Chris. "Okay, don't drown. I need to call someone."

My legs go out from under me, and I slide down the wall, my ass hitting the cold tiles with a splat. I try to laugh, but it's all too hard. My body craves sleep.

Chris

My phone is pressed to my ear, and I know I'm going to be in the worst trouble over this. Time moves so slowly for the humans. How am I supposed to remember that yesterday was her birthday, and that she'd be susceptible to the races? The phone is ringing and ringing, and I wonder if I've dialed the right number when a bored Felton finally answers.

"What?"

"What!"

"Keep yer knickers on! What do you want, Eruaphadion?"

No one knows about the chosen one, so I have to be tactful. "If someone has angel poisoning... a human... how would you fix it?"

"Let them die."

Felton is fae, and faes have no love for the humans who have poisoned their homes and almost driven out the magic from this realm. Most of them live in England where magic has flourished. In New York City, there are only pockets that still exist, and soon they will all have to leave here, or they'll die. They have created another realm to survive, but it's linked to this city, and soon, it too, shall perish and die.

"I can't, this one is..." I sigh and decide to go with a partial truth. "My friend."

"*You* have a *human* friend?"

"Yes. She's my best friend."

"Best friend? You even sound like one of them. You've been here too long. You need—"

"Felton, please. I'll *owe* you."

Felton chuckles. "Ohhh, I like the sound of that. You need to cover her with mint and honey, then pour milk over her... in that order."

"Thank you, Felton."

"She must be a special human. What's an angel doing with her—"

I hang up on him for I know I've already said too much. If the head of my troupe finds out about this, I'll be in so much more trouble than I already am. Running into Angelica's kitchen, I find milk, honey, but no mint. I have no choice but to take her with me. I can't leave the apartment for if I do, I won't be able to get back in. I head back into the bathroom and shake her roughly.

"Wake up, Ange!"

"Chrisss?"

"Yes, Ange. We're going on a road trip."

"Cool, let me grab my b-bag."

I bend down and pick her up. For me, she weighs no more than a feather. I walk back into the kitchen and lay her on the table, emptying out her handbag. I put the milk and honey into it. The honey is sticky, so I know she'll yell at me later as this is her favorite handbag, one of the few gifts she's received from Drew, and he got it for free from Hermes. If Ange had any idea how much it was worth, she would have sold it. She just thought it was pretty and a knock-off.

I place the bag over my shoulder, pick Ange up, and head for the door, all the while chanting, *cover, cover, cover.*

It's a risk that some of the races will see me, but I have to take the chance. I can't let her die. For me, it's quicker to run down the stairs than wait for the elevator. When I hit the street, I do a quick surveillance and can only see humans. None of them will notice me. I keep chanting, go into the grocery store on the corner, and take all of their mint— dried, powdered, fresh, and some in a tube. Then, I steal two cartons of milk and another container of honey. I stuff the lot into her handbag and keep moving. The only place I can think of to take her that might be secluded is Central Park. There are places within it where very few humans go. The other races are more likely to be there, but I have to take the chance.

A swooshing sound goes past me, and I look up to see the archangel, Tristan, flying by, looking for something. No doubt it's Angelica.

So, he's the bastard who poisoned her.

Bloody angels!

They think they're the chosen race.

I scoff and chant louder, *the angel will not find us.* He's only looking for Ange, and my scent and spell should confuse him. When I get to the gates of Central Park, Tristan is standing there scanning the crowd. If I get too close to him, he will sense her. He'll know she's there.

"Chrisss, I don't f-feel good."

"Ange, I need you to be quiet. Can you do that?"

She nods, but I know the closer we get to Tristan, the more dangerous this will become.

Ange will want him to find her, and if he does, she may give herself over to the choir. I can't allow that even if it means she dies.

Tristan walks toward me as if sensing us, but something catches his eye, and he takes two steps to the left. I use this distraction to run as fast as I can into the park. I glance over my shoulder, and he's turned around, but he's not following us. Tristan is concentrating hard, trying to see through my spell. A group of humans move and block his line of sight.

I use this to increase my speed and take her further into the park.

Cardinal
Angelica

My back is sore. I groan and lift my arm, everything feels weird. I touch my face and drag a hand down it. My face feels sticky and something else? I open my eyes and look at my hand, it's shiny and covered in leaves? Slowly, I sit up. I'm naked, lying on the ground, covered in something tacky. Soaking wet. And mint? I can smell mint.

"What the hell?"

"You're awake!"

I look over at Chris who's sitting on a log, looking at me anxiously.

"What the fuck, Chris?"

"How do you feel?"

"Why am I naked?" I ask, covering my bits as best I can.

"I didn't want to get anything on your robe. You're all sticky."

I look at him with distaste and arch an eyebrow. "Chris?"

"Right, right, you probably don't remember anything." Chris stands and holds my robe out to me.

"Are we're in a park? Am I naked... in a park?" I shriek at him.

Chris smirks, and when I stare daggers at him, he covers his mouth with his hand.

"There is much I need to tell you. But how about we get you home and cleaned up first?"

"Did I drink too much for my birthday? Is that why I'm here? And turn around."

Chris immediately spins to face the other direction, and I try very hard to get to my feet. My legs, they don't want to work properly, and getting my robe on over this sticky mess isn't easy.

When I've got myself sufficiently covered, I walk in front of Chris. "Where are we?"

"Central Park."

I nod at him and raise my eyebrows. "Friends don't let friends get so wasted they end up naked in Central Park. It's like a law or something."

Chris laughs, and I pin him with a look, and he quickly stops. "Sorry. You weren't in your right frame of mind. How do you feel now?"

"Sticky." I look down at my bare feet. "And minty." I look back up at him.

"Let's get you home. There's a lot, my friend, that we need to discuss."

"I don't have a headache. Did someone slip me something?"

Chris barks out a laugh. "Almost, but not quite."

I narrow my eyes at him, but he begins to walk away from me with my bag over his shoulder.

"Slow down. I don't have shoes on. And how are we going to get home? No cabbie is going to pick me up looking like this."

Chris stops and looks at me. "My place is closer. We could go there, and I promise to explain everything once you're cleaned up."

"You're lucky I love you and that you're my best friend." I'm tiptoeing toward him, being careful not to step on anything sharp. "Where did I leave my shoes?" I ask, arms extended.

Chris stops and takes his sneakers off. "Here, put these on."

"And what if you step on something sharp? Hmmm? Then what?"

"Trust me when I tell you... I'll be fine." He's smiling at me as though I'm an indulgent child, but I'm not going to look a gift horse in the mouth. So I slip his shoes on that are two sizes too big, do them up, and start walking.

Chris falls in beside me and guides me out of the park.

CHAPTER FIVE

Janardan

My feet touch solid ground, so I open my eyes and find four witches standing in front of me. I click my tongue and look at my fingernails as though they are the most boring creatures on the planet.

"Are you done?" I ask

"Janardan, we apologize. It wasn't our intent to insult or harm you, merely to read you," states one of them.

She's pretty, dark hair up in a tight bun. And she has one of those figures where she's small up top but rounded quite nicely at the bottom. I'm guessing she's in her mid-twenties, but you can never be too careful with witches. They can fool most.

"So, I can go?"

She nods. "Except it's daylight."

I step toward her, and the other three witches move back and begin to chant.

"I've been here for over a day. Why?" I ask as I tower over her.

Sweat beads on the top of her lip, so I know she's scared, but she doesn't move backward. Instead, she looks up at me.

"My name is Evie. I'm the head of the coven. We asked Baracus to bring you to us as you've ignored all of our hails."

My fangs extend, and she gasps. "Ahh, yes, Baracus. Where is he?" I ask, looking around.

"He had no idea what we were going to do to you, and we've taken the day from him. So, you see, Baracus doesn't know what he's done."

"But I know." I smile, raise my hand to touch her face only to feel a barrier separating us. I run my hand down it, and it tingles to the touch but won't let me anywhere near the witch.

Exasperated, I step back and charge the barrier only to be thrown across the room. The other three witches chant louder, and I snarl in anger at them.

"Please, Janardan! The chosen one is here."

"Here? As in, here… in this room?" I ask, scanning the faces of the witches opposite me.

One is older with long gray hair, the one next to her has red ringlets, and the other's hair is a mixture

Kathleen Kelly

of colors, but all are too old to be this socalled chosen one.

"Are you the chosen one?"

Evie laughs and shakes her head. "No. She's not here. She's—"

"Wait, wait, let me guess. She's among us, somewhere out in the world." I wave my hands in the air and turn my back to her. "The last time one of your coven sent for me over this bullshit, I ended her. Shall I do the same to you?"

The ring on my finger burns white-hot, and nausea overcomes me, forcing me to my knees.

I feel a hand on my shoulder and look up at Evie. "This time, I swear to you, it's not a trick. She could free you from your torment," says Evie, staring at my ring.

Unable to stand or move, I retract my fangs and concentrate on breathing. Something else we vampires do very well is locking in on our prey's scent, and I'm doing that now as I inhale the aromas from the four women in the room.

"The ring will stop if you stop planning to kill us," says one of the other witches.

"It's not that easy," I grind out as another wave hits me.

The oldest gray witch kneels in front of me and touches my face. "Make it that easy, Liberator. If you continue to try to fight it, it will kill you, and we need you."

Her touch lessens the pain. I exhale, concentrating on my breathing and not the fact I want to bleed all of them. Gradually, the nausea and burning cease. The old one is still in front of me and smiles warmly at me.

"Hello, Jan, it's been a long time."

I scent her again and rock back onto my feet. "Abigail? When did you get old?"

Abigail laughs, and through the wrinkles and gray hair, I see the young woman I once knew. "I'm at my end. The chosen one has stolen much of my magic from me."

"No!"

"It's all right, Jan. I welcome the end, if it will bring the races together. Too long have we warred and deceived and tried to rule each other. Too long have the humans suffered. When she comes into her full power and chooses her mate, I will become dust."

"I'll kill her mate then," I state simply.

Abigail stands, shaking her head. "I hope not for the signs point to you."

Abigail holds out her hands to me, and I stand. Laughter escapes me as I do a pirouette in front of her.

"Me? No, no, no. It can't be me. I've never taken a fully-fledged mate, and I have no intention of doing it now. Chosen one or not, it can't be me."

"Come, Jan, let's discuss this in a more comfortable setting. These old bones need to relax." I look into her eyes, and I can see she's tired. When Abigail takes a step, pain flashes across her features. Holding up my wrist, I drag a fang across it and hold it out to her as my blood stains their floor.

"No, Jan, the temptation is too much. I will not."

"This is madness. Take my blood, Abigail. It will not stop you from aging but will prevent the pain. Of course, for you, I'd make an exception and turn you. You only need to ask." In my very long life, I have only turned three people, and all of them are long dead.

Abigail smiles and keeps walking. "Come on, Jan. I need to sit."

"Will you consider it?" I ask.

Abigail purses her lips and nods. "If it will make you come with me. Yes, I'll consider it."

Abigail sits in a big overstuffed red velvet chair while I sit opposite her on a tan leather couch. The other three witches are in the room, standing well away from me.

"Wine?" asks Abigail.

"Yes." I look at the others. Abigail is clearly the most powerful one here, but she's not in charge of the coven. It doesn't make sense. "Why are you not the high priestess?"

"I'm dying."

"So? That one doesn't have half the magic you have. It should be you."

"Abigail stepped down five years ago when her magic began to fade. It's how we knew the chosen one was near," says Evie as she pours everyone a glass of wine.

To show respect, she serves me first, then Abigail. Abigail looks at her with much love in her eyes and smiles when she's handed the wine.

"Let me put a drop of my blood into the glass."

Abigail looks up at Evie, who frowns and looks back at me. "Only a drop. There's nothing worse than a witch with the crave."

I pierce the end of my finger with my fang and squeeze until a blood drop forms. Evie holds the glass out, and I let it fall into the wine. Because I am so old, my blood is more potent and can cure most illnesses, but it can't stop the aging process. If you have enough of it, it can slow it down. Most witches don't need it as they keep their youth with their spells and potions. To see Abigail old and frail saddens me. We were lovers once, and good friends, but that was a long time ago.

"Abigail has had my blood before. She never suffered the crave."

Evie's eyes widen, and she looks at Abigail. "Is that true?"

Abigail waves a hand in the air and takes a sip of wine. "It was before you were born. Sit, Evie, Jan will not hurt you." Abigail looks up at the other two. "Gloria, Patricia, sit. It will make all of us more comfortable."

Evie sits next to me, and I study her profile and mannerisms. It's something vampires do to better know their prey.

"This one is related to you, isn't she?" I ask.

Abigail nods. "My granddaughter. And you're right, she's not half the witch I am, but when the chosen one comes into her power, what's left of my magic will go to Evie, and she will be a force to be reckoned with."

"Why do you think I'm this chosen one's mate?" I take a sip of my wine, smiling to myself.

Abigail looks to Evie, who shifts on the couch, so she's facing me.

"Your aura. It's said that the chosen one will be bathed in cardinal. We've seen red auras before but none the color of yours," states Evie.

"This proves nothing." I sigh and stare at Abigail. "All this proves is I have a red aura." "Cardinal

red," replies Abigail.

"Fine, cardinal red. I'm a vampire, we're immortal, which could mean she's not even been born yet. You witches with your spells, you don't know everything."

"You aren't immortal, merely hard to kill. Abigail isn't the only one who's been affected. It all started when the chosen one turned twenty, and the heads of all the races felt it. Some of their life force was siphoned off and this continued until she came of age at twenty-five. For Abigail, it was her magic. The others all had similar things happen."

"Levi would have told me."

Abigail scoffs. "No, he wouldn't. Leviathan takes power from the clutch, but you've never sworn fealty to him. You, alone, could rule all vampires, but you turned your back on them after the first war." I go to speak, but Abigail holds up a hand. "Yes, yes, I know you fought in all the wars. You're the oldest and should be their sire. We believe, because of this, you are the chosen one's mate."

I cast a look at the other witches, and they are all nodding.

"Fine, let's say I am. Let's pretend the chosen one is among us. How do we find her?"

Evie answers, "She'll find you within the next month."

"So, you drag me here only to tell me that she's going to find me, anyway? I haven't fed. I'm hungry, and I've had just about enough bullshit for one day." I stand.

Abigail does so too and without pain.

I watch as she stretches and flexes, enjoying a body with no restrictions.

"Thank you, Jan."

I can't help myself, and I smile at her. "Do you want me to leave you some of my blood?"

Abigail's eyes flick to Evie, so I turn and look at her as she says, "No."

"If this prophecy is true, then your grandmother only has a month left, and one drop of my blood will not induce the crave."

The crave is something all the races have in common. It means different things to all of us. For vampires, if we crave your blood, you're as good as dead and drained. For witches, it's vampire blood which acts as an opiate on them if they have too much.

"I do feel so much better, Evie."

"Janardan, there is more we need to discuss. Although the chosen one will find you, if she couples with another of the races first, they will take her power. Only her true mate will let her blossom into—"

"Into what, Evie?" I ask impatiently.

"We don't know. We hope that as a true partnership, yours and hers, will combine to end the wars. Let humans know we're here without scaring them. End—"

"Peace on earth and goodwill to all men? Please! Fairy tales and myth." I walk over to the decanter holding the red wine, prick my finger, and let two drops of blood fall into it.

"Janardan, you have to find her first," states Abigail.

I walk toward her and hold out my hand. Lies are more easily felt if I have skin-to-skin contact. Like all supernaturals, I can normally tell when someone is lying. Witches, though, have their spells. Abigail puts her hand in mine, and I hear the other three witches gasp. They're probably worried I'm going to end her.

"If what you say is true. How do you know she's here? And how will I find her?"

"Have you felt more settled, Jan? Has the fire that once drove you to roam the earth let you settle here for over fifteen years? Do you feel like you're at home?"

I take a deep breath and ponder what she's said. The moment I set foot in New York City a sense of belonging overcame me. I bought a penthouse overlooking Central Park. And yes, this was the first time I ever felt like I had a home. The penthouse was a strange choice for me. It's quite ornate inside with high ceilings, crown moldings, and a large outside patio. I have no idea what possessed me to buy it. In the past, it was always first-floor dwellings with little light, which were easily defendable against intruders. My home during the day is bathed in daylight except for the panic room that I sleep in. This, alone, protects me from the sun and enemies who try to destroy me.

"Yes, New York City feels like home."

"Have you not noticed over the years that all of the races have their leaders here? We all feel it, feel her. As for finding her, you need to heed the signs as they will be everywhere if you let them in."

"Truth." I drop her hand and smile at her. "The truth, well, you *believe* what you're saying. It doesn't make it fact." I take a step back from Abigail, a slight frown mars her face.

"Go rest for the day. We've arranged for a feeder to be in your room. A woman, but not a very nice one. Her soul is dark," says Evie from behind me.

"You'll let me go as soon as it's night?" Abigail nods. "Would you escort me to my room?"

Abigail smiles at me affectionately. "It would be an honor."

"No!" Evie replies rather loudly.

I turn to her. "I don't feed on the innocents, you know this. I'm assuming that's why you have someone with a dark soul waiting for me."

When we are first turned, the bloodlust roars through our veins. If it's not controlled, we turn into a berserker vampire, and all the races hunt us. Too much innocent blood will do the same. My kind learned that if we drained the evil and tainted, we kept what little humanity we had left. Like a drug, innocent blood is hard to kick as it is the sweetest.

Evie huffs at me. "Right now, Abigail, my grandmother, is looking at you adoringly and wouldn't be able to stop you from draining her."

"I would, too. And besides, Jan wouldn't do that. He's always been a gentleman and lives by his own code."

I peer into Abigail's eyes. Her pupils are dilated, and she's moving freely. Evie is right, her grandmother is entranced with me.

"You're both correct." I turn to Evie. "High Priestess, I swear by this trinket on my finger that I'll not harm your grandmother. All I need is food and rest."

"Swear on your soul that you will not hurt any of the witches here in our coven."

"I swear on my soul that for the next twenty-four hours, I'll not harm any witch in this coven." Evie narrows her gaze and nods. "After that, you're all fair game."

Abigail laughs and links her arm with mine. "Oh, Jan, you had to ruin it."

"You all seem to forget this ring keeps me in line whether I want it to or not."

CHAPTER SIX

Angelica

It's the weirdest thing. Chris won't let me touch him. I had a shower, and it took forever to get my hair clean. After, when I came out and went to wrap my arms around him, he yelped and stepped out of my reach. I'm in one of his tracksuits, which is way too big for me, sitting on his gray couch with my feet tucked up under me. Chris keeps glancing at me as he makes us both a cup of tea.

This too is weird. Chris *never* drinks tea, only coffee. When he finally gets it all done, he puts the cups on a tray and places them before me on the coffee table. Chris doesn't even sit next to me but sits in an armchair across from me.

"Did I make a pass at you last night?" I blurt out.
"What? No!"

"Okay, phew!" I laugh awkwardly. "The last thing I remember is leaving work on Thursday. After that, it's all a bit of a blur."

"Today is Saturday."

"What? It can't be!"

"Yeah, it is. Ange, you know how on most days I like to hold your hand and do that little blessing thing for luck?"

"Yes." I giggle. "It's one of your little quirks. But I don't mind it."

"See, I try to remember to do it every day so that we have some human contact."

"Okay."

"I missed it on Thursday, and Thursday was your birthday." Chris is staring at his hands that are clasped together in front of him.

"You forgot my birthday. I remember I took in cupcakes, and you didn't even wish me a happy birthday. You just laughed, stole one, and ran away. And no, you didn't do your blessing. It was so busy at work that I hardly saw you all day."

Chris raises his eyes to meet mine. "I'm going to tell you something, and I need you to promise me you won't be mad."

"Oh my God, did you have sex with me while I was passed out?"

"No! No, I wouldn't do *that*," replies Chris earnestly.

I laugh nervously and take a sip of my tea. It's peppermint.

"Tell me whatever it is. I'm sure we can work through it."

"You were born at ten o'clock at night, precisely. You weighed exactly eight pounds, and your mother left you in a shelter."

I frown at him. "Did you run a background check on me?"

"Sort of. I'm from an organization called the troupe. We seek out special... children and keep a watch over them. It was pure chance that one of us found you. I was assigned to you when you moved to New York City."

I put down my cup. "You were assigned to me?"

"I know how it sounds. I need you to know I've never lied to you. I've only ever protected you and tried to be your friend."

I put my feet on the floor. "Someone is paying you to be my friend?" I whisper.

"No! No, I don't get paid. It's an honor and a privilege to be with you." Chris moves to sit near me on the couch, and I shuffle further away.

"I don't understand. I'm a nobody."

Chris laughs. He reaches for my hand and pulls back, frowning. "Do you trust me?"

"I did." I look down at my hands. "Chris, did you give me something? Is that how I ended up naked in the park?"

The thought of him hurting me is terrifying, more so as I'm sitting in his apartment, alone.

"God, no! No, no, no!" Chris shuffles further away from me, then stands and runs his hands through his hair. "Goddammit!" Chris stalks to a window looking out. "It wasn't supposed to be like this." He sighs and drops his head into his hands. "There's a process. I screwed up."

"Chris, is that your real name? What were you supposed to do with me?"

"Christopher is a variation of my name in English. Easy for you to say." Chris turns and faces me. "The head of my troupe said I'd feel unparalleled devotion to you, and that as soon as I realized you had ascended, I should contact him." Chris shakes his head and laughs bitterly. "Too late for that. I think I was devoted to you the day you bought me a coffee at work for no other reason than you liked me. It's been a long time since someone has done something for me for no reason. The races normally always want something or want you to do something in return. My appointment to you was to appease my father." Chris waves his hand in the air. "All of this is moot. Ask me anything, and I'll answer."

"How did I end up naked in the park?"

"An angel, I think it was Tristan, poisoned you. If he'd been able to have sex with you, he'd be your chosen mate. The poisoning happens by accident, you must have wanted to have sex with him, but for some reason, you didn't do the deed. He's been searching for you."

I can tell he believes everything he just told me. Now, I'm scared.

"Did he take me to the park?"

"No. I went to your apartment yesterday as you missed work. You let me in. I realized you'd turned twenty-five, you smelled like angel, then you got sick. I phoned a friend, and he told me how to cure you. I needed to smother you in honey, mint, and milk. I couldn't leave you in your apartment as I wouldn't have been able to get back in. So, the closest safe place for you and me was the park. I know all the secret places."

I stand and take a few paces toward the front door.

"Okay, so let me get this straight. An angel poisoned me. You took me naked to the park and covered me in honey and mint."

"And milk."

"Right, and milk. Why didn't anyone stop you?"

"Oh, I put a spell on us so no one could see us."

"Right." I keep backing away from him until my back hits the door. I reach down and grab the handle.

"It's not safe for you out there. If you happen to brush up against a supernatural, you'll reveal their true face. They'll either know you're the chosen one or think you're a half-breed. Either way, it'll be bad for you."

I smile at him and twist the handle. In a blur, Chris is in front of me.

"I know, I'm scaring you. I promise to let you go, but first, I need you to touch me."

"Eww! Chris! Have you taken something? This isn't you," I yell.

Chris smiles and shakes his head.

"Not like that. Let's just shake hands."

Chris holds out his hand, and I tentatively extend my hand to him.

"Don't freak out like last time."

"What?"

"We've done this once before. You didn't handle it well. Remember, I'm your friend and humble servant."

I smack my lips together and place my hand in his. Slowly, he morphs into a taller being with pointy ears and long dark hair. His eyes are a deep chocolate brown, and he is beautiful, breathtaking to look at. Nothing like he looked before.

"Did you drug me again?"

Chris smiles, and it's glorious.

"No, chosen one. You have no idea how long I've waited for this day. There have been many over the years that we thought would transform, but I'm lucky enough to have the real thing."

I pull my hand out of his. "Holy shit," I whisper.

"Indeed."

"Can I go home now?"

"You see me for what I am, and you want to leave? I've gotta say, Ange, I thought you'd be more..."

"More what?"

"I thought you'd have more questions or yell at me... or I don't know anything else, but this. Do you understand what I've told you? Talk to me, Ange."

"I'm tired."

"You slept for a really long time. You snored even."

"Chris, p-please let me go."

Hearing the fear in my voice, Chris backs up several feet. "You're scared of me."

He's right. I am. I'm terrified my friend has slipped me something and is now having a complete mental breakdown.

"I want to go home."

"Go. But Ange, try not to touch anyone. Go straight home. Be careful, and if you need me, please ring. No supernatural can get into your home unless you specifically invite them in. You have to say the words. Do you understand?"

I cock my head to the side. "You're letting me go?"

"Yes. I have one piece of advice. Heed the signs. They will be all around you. Follow your instincts, and if you need me, call my name, and I'll be there."

"So, I don't need to ring you?"

Chris chuckles and shrugs. "Either way, I'm your protector."

"Right." I fake a smile, open the door, slip out into the hallway and quickly pull it shut.

With fear pumping through my veins, I run to the elevator and out onto the street, and I keep going until my lungs burn. People yell and curse at me as I pass them by, but no one stops me. Tears cloud my vision as I realize my best friend has gone completely insane and that he may have drugged me.

I stop, doubled over as I suck in air, hands on my knees, shaking my head, and wondering what the hell has happened.

"You all right, honey?" asks an elderly woman.

I nod, then shake my head and look up at her. She reaches out and touches my face.

I straighten up, and the old lady melts into a hideous creature. Her skin hangs from her body, and she has tusks.

"You're a fucking half-breed? Should have known. Don't look at me. For fuck's sake, stop staring. I'm not as young as I used to be. I can't project forever." The woman or beast or whatever she is, snarls at me and walks away. Just as she gets to the street corner, she turns and gives me the bird.

"Are you okay?" asks Chris.

I jump, clutching my chest. "What the fuck was that?"

"Demon, an old one. You don't see too many of the old ones. They prey on the bitter humans or the ones who are vulnerable."

Chris is looking into the crowd in the direction the thing went.

"Are you following me?"

"Yes. I'm making sure you get home okay. I promise I wasn't going to let her hurt you."

I follow his gaze and see a red bird sitting on top of a sign. It appears as though the bird is staring at me.

"Do you see that?" I ask.

"See what?"

"The bird on top of that sign?"

"No. But if you do, you should act on it."

"What do you mean?"

"The demon flipped you off, the bird, and now you're seeing a red bird I can't see. Follow it."

"Fuck you, Chris," I hiss. "And stop following me."

Chris sighs. "Okay, here's the thing. I have to do as you say, but I can't let you run around unprotected, so if you tell me to stop following you, I have to enlist the help of someone else. Do you understand?"

"No, I don't understand a fucking thing. I don't understand how my best friend could have drugged me and done God knows what. I thought we were friends." A sob escapes me, and I feel like the world is pressing in on me.

Chris nods and takes a few steps back. "Can you still see the bird?"

I look back at the sign, and it's gone, so I shake my head.

"Damn." Chris holds out my handbag. "You left this behind. Go home, Ange, and if you feel like talking, you know how to find me."

Chris smiles then fades away. I wave a hand where he was standing, but there's nothing there, just my bag on the ground. I open it up but there's nothing inside it. It's empty.

I pick it up and put it on my shoulder then head for home. I'm not running this time, only power walking. Most people move out of my way as I'm sure I look crazed. I'm careful not to touch anyone. I have no idea if Chris is telling me the truth or not, but I have no intention of seeing another demon.

When I reach my apartment, I realize I don't have my keys. I sigh in frustration and hope the door is unlocked

"Please?" I say to the ceiling as I try the handle. It turns, and I push open my door. Grace is sitting in the hallway looking at me with her golden eyes. "Is it safe? Has anyone come in while I've been gone?" Grace says nothing, only looks at me. I tentatively take a step into my apartment. I'm listening for intruders. I hear nothing, so I close the door. I search my bedroom, bathroom, and the rest of the place. There's no one here. I run back to my bedroom and look under the bed, no one's hiding.

With a sigh, I go back to my front door and lock it. Grace is weaving in and out of my legs, purring.

"Are you hungry? I'm starving. Let's get ourselves something to eat."

As I head for the kitchen, Grace runs ahead of me and stops in front of her bowl.

"I know, it's coming," I say to her. In response, I get a long, loud meow. "Keep your voice down, I've had a weird day."

Not really caring about me, Grace continues to cry until I've put food in her bowl. After I've fed her, I go back into my bedroom, strip off, and take a very long, hot shower.

I'm sitting on my bed when my phone goes off. I look at the screen, and it's a message from Chris.

Chris: *Are you ok?*

I stare at the screen, and the message fades away.
Are you ok? No, I don't think I am.

And Chris is the person I'd call to talk to about all of this, and he's, he's not what he seems. Even if I believe him and his troupe, he lied to me for years. How do I get past that?

Standing, I look out the window. It's dark outside, but New York City is never truly dark. Lights illuminate the streets, and I look down at the people scurrying below. It's Saturday night, and I would normally be going out to dinner with Chris or on a date, not that I date a lot. I turn my back against the window and walk to my closet.

I pull out my favorite pair of blue jeans, a black shirt, and a pair of black leather knee-high boots. I sit in front of my dressing table and stare at myself. I look the same, but it feels like my whole world is upside down. I brush my hair and put my long blonde locks up in a high ponytail, then use my curling iron to give it a bit of bounce on the ends. It looks okay. Next, I apply a small amount of foundation, eyeliner, and mascara, and then, I put some gloss on my lips. When I finish, I admire myself in the mirror.

"You look good. Now, let's go face the world outside and see if we spot any more monsters."

I go back into the kitchen where the contents of my bag are strewn across the dining table. I open my bag and place my wallet inside but pull my hand back out quickly as I touch something sticky.

"Goddammit, Chris," I mutter as I pull the wallet back out and go wash my hands. "Well, that's just great."

Cardinal

I go back into my closet and grab an old black bag. It's the size of an A4 sheet of paper with a wrist strap hanging off it. It's plain and not as nice as my other bag or as big, but it will do.

Wiping off my wallet, I put it into my bag, grab my keys, give Grace a pat, and walk toward the front door. When I open it, there's a policeman standing on the other side.

"Hello?"

"Hello, Angelica. How are you feeling?"

"I'm sorry, do I know you?"

He feels familiar but also not at the same time. Maybe he has one of those faces where you think you know him, but he only looks similar to someone you know. To clear my mind, I shake my head.

"I'm Officer Tristan Saint. We met last night."

He smiles at me, and I feel like I know him, but there's something inside me telling me to be careful.

"We did? Last night is a bit of a blur."

"I took you to the hospital. You weren't yourself. Could I come in?"

"I'm about to go out."

"It won't take a minute, just need to ask you a couple of questions."

With a sigh, I stand to one side and gesture for him to come in. Officer Saint grins at me, but he doesn't come into my home.

"Officer?"

"Oh, so I can come in?"

I nod and make another sweeping gesture with my arm. "The door's open."

"Right, so invite me in."

I frown at him, and Chris' words come back to me, *he needs to be invited in*. I cock my head to the side and stare at the officer.

"You can't, can you?"

"Of course, I can. Just say the words." Officer Saint nods and grins at me expectantly.

"The door is open."

"Say the words."

"Right. That's how it works for you... you supernaturals. Doesn't it?"

"Ma'am, I have no idea what you're talking about."

There's something in his tone, and I've moved further into my apartment, but he's not making a move to enter.

"So that's why you're out there, and I'm in here."

"Because you haven't invited me in." I laugh, and his handsome face scowls at me. "Ask me in." "Chris," I yell.

I see a blur then my friend, Chris, in his elvin form appears behind Officer Saint.

"You called?"

"What is he, Chris?"

Tristan turns to frown at Chris. "Don't."

"He's an angel. An archangel. Very powerful, but not so powerful that he can enter your home without an invitation."

"You know what she is, don't you, elf? Do you want her for yourself? Is that it?" sneers Officer Saint.

"Eww! No! I'm her protector and most importantly, *her friend*."

"If I come out into the hall, can he hurt me, Chris?"

"No, of course, I won't," replies Officer Saint quickly.

"Stay where you are. Tristan here can't get to you, but if you come out here, he can do as he wishes. Angels are so fickle."

Tristan frowns and slams his fist into the plaster beside my door. "Let. Me. In," he roars.

"Chris, please come in," I say quickly.

I feel wind rush past me, and when I turn around, Chris is sitting on my couch, smiling at me.

"Shut the door and come join me. A coffee would be nice."

I push the door shut and go into my kitchen, putting on the coffee machine.

"So, he was an actual angel?"

"Yes. Are you okay?"

"I'm glad you told me about inviting them in."

Chris chuckles and flicks his long dark hair over his shoulder. "You're mine to protect." Chris walks toward me, frowning. "Why do you look like you're about to go out?"

"I'm hungry. I was going to go out for dinner."

"Oh! Where? I'm starved, too. I've been waiting on your call. Why haven't you returned my texts?"

"Maybe because I'm mad at you, and you've lied to me for years," I reply sarcastically.

"Right, that. You humans are so sensitive."

"Do you want a coffee or not?"

Chris smiles, and it's like his whole being lights up.

"Yes, please. I think I want Chinese for dinner. How about you?"

"Sounds like a plan."

I finish making him and myself a coffee, and I notice Chris hasn't approached me. He's keeping some distance between us.

"Are you staying away from me to make me feel safer?"

Chris nods. "You were scared of me before. I didn't like it."

I nod. Chris is right, I was scared. I cast a look at my front door. "Do you think he's still there?"

"Probably. You're a prize he won't want to lose."

"If I touch him, can he pull me out of my home?"

"Yes, he can, but we could make him promise not to. If he wants to claim you as badly as I think he does, he'll agree. Angels don't break their promises."

I puff out my cheeks and let out a sigh. "Okay, you do the promising thing, and I'll do the touching."

"Sounds kinky."

I shake my head at Chris and smile, his return smile making him more handsome.

"Have you always been this attractive?"

Laughter escapes him. "Yes, Ange, but you aren't my type."

"Oh, I never thought of you as gay."

Chris laughs harder. "No! Human! I don't do humans. I'm promised to an elvin princess."

"You're promised?"

"All this for another time." Chris stalks past me and opens the door. Tristan is standing on the other side, looking angry. "Shall we?"

"Shall we what?" asks Tristan.

"By the grace of your wings, we want you to promise that you will not abduct Angelica from her home when she reaches out to touch you."

"Why would I promise that?" Tristan's blond eyebrows knit together in a frown.

"If you want me to trust you and be your friend, you'll promise," I interject.

Both men look at me, Chris with a bemused smile and Tristan with a frown.

"Fine," replies Tristan dejectedly.

"Not so fast... say the words," says Chris smugly.

"By the grace of my wings, I promise not to abduct you from your home when you, Angelica, reach out to touch me. How was that?"

Chris winks at me and says, "You could have sounded a little bit more sincere, but it will do. Come, Ange, touch the angel!" Chris does jazz hands toward Tristan, and I giggle.

Tentatively, I reach out and touch Tristan on the hand, slowly, he morphs into a glowing angel. He's breathtaking.

"You're so, so..." "What?"

asks Tristan.

"Pretty," I whisper.

Tristan smiles and rubs the back of his head. "Pretty?" He links his fingers with mine.

"No, that's not right, you are beautiful to look at, but you're manly like a Greek god."

"Come with me, Angelica. Let me show you how beautiful this world can be."

Tristan's voice is like silk. It washes over you, and when he smiles, he glows brighter. I find myself leaning toward him.

"Okay, that's enough. Back it up, big guy," yells Chris.

"Eruaphadion! Let her choose," exclaims Tristan.

Chris jerks me back, and the spell is broken.

I feel warm, fuzzy, and a little turned on. "How did you do that?" I ask.

"Do what?" asks Tristan with a smirk.

I look at Chris, his eyebrows raise knowingly.

"Did you know he could do that?"

"The angels are a delectable race. They know how to twist all of us to their wishes, but they can also be scary. God's hitmen, so to speak." "God? There's a god?" I ask.

Tristan scoffs, and Chris grins.

"A conversation for another time," replies Chris as he shuts the door.

I walk into my bedroom and notice a red ribbon hanging off my mirror. It's been there forever, but I undo it and tie it in my hair.

"Are you okay?"

"How did he do that?" I'm staring at myself in the mirror. "If he'd asked me, I think I'd have let him take me anywhere."

"They are divine creatures. Blessed. They can get good people to do just about anything, and they are horny bastards."

I burst out laughing and stare at Chris in the mirror.

"Well, that explains that. How do we go out for dinner if he's waiting at my front door?" Chris smiles. "More promises."

Angelica doesn't realize it, but after Tristan touched her, she gravitated toward the red ribbon. Tying it in her hair is also odd for her. Hell, even putting it up in a ponytail is weird. Ange typically leaves it down and straight. The curls are odd too.

Tristan definitely has a hold on her, but the ribbon, that's something else. I leave Ange in her bedroom and go back out to Tristan.

"I need you to make a few oaths to protect Angelica and the process."

"Have you told the troupe yet, Eruaphadion? I don't see any imperial guards here."

"I want what's best for Angelica. The troupe, like you, would want her for her power. Right now, no one knows what that means. If the prophecy is correct, her true power will come into play when she meets her mate."

"How do you know that isn't me?"

"She's only attracted to you when you touch her. Angelica doesn't feel the pull toward you. When she meets the one, she will. There will be nothing we can do to stop it."

Tristan nods. "What do you want of me?"

"You're going to swear to leave her alone."

Tristan shakes his head. "I will not!"

I raise my hands. "You will for one day. That's all I'm going to get you to swear to. I need a day to prepare her. Angelica knows nothing of the supernaturals, and she needs to be warned."

"Warned?"

I nod. Tristan gives me his back and looks up as though he's praying, then turns around and nods once. "I'll give you twenty-four hours to the second, and then I'm coming for her, and you had better stay out of my way, *elf*."

Tristan spreads out his gorgeous, white wings, blinding me with light, then disappears. Typical angels, all show.

CHAPTER
SEVEN

Janardan

The witches kept their word, and as soon as night crept into the sky, I was released. I didn't see anyone as I made my way out of their stronghold. I'm sure they were watching me, but no one, not even Abigail, wished me goodbye.

When I emerge out onto the street, it's not the alley but the middle of Central Park. I turn around, but there's no door, only trees. I chuckle to myself, witches and their spells. I breathe in the night—the air in the park always smells good, a combination of earth and greenery.

I walk a few paces, then a scent hits my nose. I double back and find a place where someone had lain. The smell of mint, honey, and bad milk hit my senses, but underneath it is another scent. Angel? Then underneath that, someone else. Female, delightful, my fangs extend, but I'm not hungry. This is something else. Lust, longing things I haven't felt in nearly twenty years.

Honing in on that scent, I follow it. It takes me to a building, but I can smell that she left here and ventured away from it. There's also the scent of elf in the air. He's either with her or following her. My blood begins to boil, the thought of someone else touching her makes me angry. I stop in my tracks. I do not even know this woman, so why would I care? Shaking my head, I turn and head for my home.

I am too old to be blinded by the crave. I haven't craved a person since my early days. Why the instinct has kicked in now is anybody's guess. Perhaps the witches have cast a spell on me? All their talk about me being the chosen one's mate must be rubbing off on me.

I keep walking, and when I look up, I've doubled back and have honed in on her scent again. I growl at myself in frustration. People around me give me a wide berth, no one makes eye contact. I look up at the heavens and see an angel fly by. They told me to look out for signs. Angels are pure, right? So maybe my intentions are pure? With a shake of my head, I continue on. I am old enough to control myself. I only fed a few hours ago, so I should be fine. The scent is so sweet, full of life and mischief.

Soon, I'm standing in front of the same building. I go up in the elevator but have to stop on each floor to find where she got off. When I step out onto the third floor, elf and angel mingle with her scent. Her scent is overpowering around a door—this must be her home. I knock on it, listening for the sounds of life behind it, but I get nothing. Whomever she is, she's not home.

With a frustrated growl, I turn and go back to the elevator where there are two of them, and her scent is much fresher in this one. I go back down to the ground level and follow the scent. It's hers and an elf. Lycan washes over me, and I realize I'm not the only one hunting the woman.

I quicken my pace and almost run into the lycan. He's taller than me and has more bulk. He surrounds me, snarling, his dark features twisting as he bares his teeth.

"Not here, dog. You need to remember where you are."

"You're hunting her, too?" he growls.

"Her scent is... compelling."

The lycan nods and regains some composure. "Who else do you think is hunting her?"

"Is that what we're doing?" I ask, frowning.

He points to a woman in the crowd, hair up high in a ponytail, red ribbon blowing in the breeze.

"She wears the color to attract us…" He pauses. "I've never felt the urge so great. Not in all my years."

Most of the lore surrounding the supernatural community has some basis in truth. The little red riding hood story talks about a little girl on her way to grandma's house wearing a red cloak. It's the red that attracts the lycans. I've seen the pack surround their queens in red, and it sends the males into an erotic frenzy.

"I'm Janardan." I hold out my hand to him, and he raises his eyebrows in surprise.

"The Janardan?"

I chuckle. "Just Janardan."

"I'm Hunter, alpha of the pack."

Now it's my turn to be surprised. It's not often the alpha is out on his own. I search the crowd around me and cannot see any of his pack, but I'm not stupid enough to believe he'd be alone.

"Where did you first come across her scent?"

"I was in a restaurant with the pack about a mile back, and it wafted in on the breeze. You?"

"Central Park."

Hunter grins at me and rocks back on his heels. "Shall we flip a coin?"

My fangs extend, and he growls at me.

"The woman is mine. I scented her first." "I saw her first," counters Hunter.

I take two steps back and size up my opponent. Hunter is formidable, but he's no match for me. A growl from behind me lets me know that there are more of them. I let my senses wash over the crowd—there are ten lycans advancing on us.

"You can't defeat all of us. We could overwhelm you. Let this one go."

I shake my head, let my fingernails extend, and assume a fighting stance. Hunter growls, his upper and lower teeth extend, and his nails, like mine, become long, pointy claws.

I'm about to launch myself at him when a small red bird lands on my shoulder. Hunter flicks his gaze to it. I go to brush it off, and another lands on my other shoulder. They are the size of mice, so tiny and red. They are chirping loudly at Hunter.

"What the fuck?" Hunter growls, his voice no longer sounding human.

"Can you see them, too?" asks a female.

Her scent hits me, and my nostrils flare. *It's her.* Hunter takes a step toward her, and I snarl.

"Get back, dog!"

Hunter ignores me and takes another step. An elf appears, and he's mad which, for an elf, is an unusual thing. They normally hold their emotions close to their chests. I've only ever seen two elves in my very long life lose their tempers. This one makes three. I breathe deeply and realize he's the one who's been with the woman this whole time.

"Is she yours?" I ask him.

He flicks his gaze to me. "Mine to protect." He scans the crowd and looks at Hunter. "Tell them to get back. I'll defend her with my life. The pack can't afford another war with the troupe, your numbers are depleted after the last battle you lost. Think, alpha!"

"What makes you think the troupe would go to war over one measly elf?" sneers Hunter.

"I'm Eruaphadion, son of Aran. Tangle with me at your peril."

I cock my head and take in this elf. *Son of Aran?* Aran is the name of the head of the troupe or their king. The leader of the troupe loses his birth name and becomes Aran. All the kings of the elvin have been called this for as long as any can remember. It's also one of the reasons humans believe that elves are immortal. They aren't, but they do live for hundreds of years.

Eruaphadion has positioned himself in front of the woman, staff in hand, situated in a fighter's stance. He's taller than both of us, long dark hair pulled back off his face, and he's focused on Hunter.

The woman peers over his shoulder at me and smiles. My fangs and claws instantly retract, and I take in her appearance. She's curvy, blonde, young, and has these amazing green eyes that feel like they see right into my soul.

I glance at Hunter, and he too has regained his human form. The elf, though, has not relaxed. He moves slightly to the left, so he's blocking Hunter's view, but in doing so, I can see her completely.

She's wearing jeans, boots, and a black shirt. Nothing out of the ordinary, yet I find her to be the most desirable woman I've ever laid eyes on.

"What are you?" I ask her.

"Human."

I take a step toward her and am hit in the chest once and quickly with the elf's staff.

"Back up!"

"I give you my word, I'll not harm her."

"Janardan, liberator of the cycle of life and death, do you really think I can trust *you?*"

"You know me?"

"All fear the dark because of you, Liberator. Many of my kind have been lost to you. If it weren't for the truce of the last great war, I'd end you."

"Chris!" The elf glances at her but doesn't stand down. "That's enough. Ending people! This isn't who you are."

"Angelica, run," demands Eruaphadion.

"I will not!" She peers around the elf and looks from Hunter to me. "Swear to Chris and me you will not hurt me, and he'll stop acting like a... like a... overprotective, pointy-eared jerk!"

I burst out laughing, and so does the lycan.

"I promise I won't hurt you."

Hunter also says, "I promise I won't hurt you or the pointy-eared jerk."

I chuckle, and so does she, then she walks around Chris and comes within touching distance of me. I want so badly to reach out to her, but I hold myself still. She touches the elf's staff and pushes it down.

"Stand down, Captain War Pants. They've sworn to be good."

"There are still more lycans in the crowd."

Angelica tilts her head to the side and looks around. She takes a few steps toward me and stares me in the eyes. "Is that true?"

"The lycans aren't mine to control, but yes, little one, there are more in the crowd. You should get Hunter here to tell them to stand down."

Kathleen Kelly

Angelica smiles at me and nods, then looks at the lycan. "Hunter, could you please ask your people to stand down?"

"Stand down," yells Hunter instantly.

The humans in the crowd give him strange looks, but the lycans in the crowd stop circling and walk toward us. I instinctively put myself between her and the pack.

"I'm warning you, Liberator, stand back from my... friend," says the elf.

"Friend?" I look at Angelica, and she nods.

"Yes, we're friends."

"He's the king's son, and you're... what are you?" I ask as I lean in and sniff her.

"Did you just smell me?" Angelica looks around me to the elf. "Is that a thing? Do all you supernatural types sniff one another like dogs do?" She looks up at me. "Keep away from my butt."

I bark out a laugh. She's placed her hands on her hips and looks quite serious.

"Not a dog." I point at Hunter. "He might sniff your butt, but not me."

"*You* sniffed me!"

I laugh at her and shake my head. "You're a curious little thing. And I don't sniff, I scent."

"Same thing," Angelica replies with no small amount of sass.

"And we all know once vampires have your scent, you're as good as dead," replies Hunter.

"That's a lie," I state.

"Oh, really? It's common knowledge that vampires track their prey by scent," says the elf, cockily.

I look down at Angelica and pull the ribbon out of her hair, then put it in my pocket. She frowns at me then notices the birds on my shoulders.

"Are they real?"

Both the birds have gone silent and appear to be rubbing themselves on the tops of my shoulders.

"It would appear so," I say as I try to shoo them away.

They merely fly upward then land back on my shoulders.

"Weird," says Angelica.

She holds out her finger, and one of them flies onto it.

"Oh my God, I'm like Snow White!"

I laugh at her, and she holds out her other hand, and the other bird hops onto it. Hunter moves to stand next to me.

"What does it mean?" he asks.

"We need a witch," I reply.

"Wait, wait, wait! There are witches, too? How many races are there?" asks Angelica.

"You don't know?" asks Hunter.

Angelica shakes her head and smiles at the little birds. They both chirp loudly at her and fly away."

"Oh!" Angelica watches them go, but I only have eyes for her.

"Ange, we should go," says the elf.

"We were going to have Chinese..." Angelica pauses and looks at Hunter, then me. "Would you like to join us?"

Hunter and I both say, "Yes."

But her protector says a very loud, "No!"

Angelica walks around me and touches the elf on the shoulder. "Okay, I might be new to all this supernatural stuff, but they can both track us, right?"

"Yes."

"Well, then they might as well come." Angelica turns around and looks directly at me. "That is, of course, if you want to. Do vampires eat?"

I smile and offer her my arm. Angelica links hers with mine and something close to an electric shock goes through my system.

"Oh!" gasps Angelica.

"Did you feel that, too?"

"Yes," her voice is breathy. "What does it mean?"

I shake my head. "I'm not sure, but let's find out."

All ten of the pack and their leader join us in the restaurant. I make sure I am sitting next to Angelica. Much to the elf's displeasure, he sits on her other side glaring at all of us.

"Can I touch you?" asks Angelica looking at me shyly.

"Of course."

She grabs my hand and closes her eyes, the electric shock surges through my system, but this time I am prepared for it.

Angelica gasps but does not let go. "Why does it do that?" Angelica asks.

I shake my head. "I don't know."

She's staring at me as if she's trying to see something. After a moment, she frowns and looks to her elvish friend, Chris.

"He looks the same."

"Janardan is a vampire."

"Yeah, but he didn't get pointy ears or fangs or anything. He just looks handsome."

I cock an eyebrow at the lycan, and he snarls.

"My turn." Hunter leans across the table and holds out his hand.

Angelica reaches for him, and I instinctively put my arm around her. They touch, and she stares at him intently.

"I'm not getting anything. No electricity. Nothing."

"Electricity?" asks the elf.

"When I touch Janardan, I get an electric shock."

The elf frowns. "No, no, no! You can't be the one. It can't be you. You're tainted, foul, and don't deserve redemption."

"I don't understand." Angelica looks from the elf to me.

The elf stands and drags her up with him. "We're going."

I stand and shake my head. "No. Let me take her to the witches. We can do a trial by combat as they did in the days of old."

"For she will come into her power on her twenty-fifth year, and when she touches the dutiful, their true selves will become known her. She will be all-powerful and guide us to redemption with her true mate and protector at her side. All will fear them as they shall rule the races."

"I'm familiar with the book and the prophecy. For more than a century, I have kept mostly to myself. I'm the oldest and should be the head of the clutch, but I have no taste for leadership. I'm no threat to you, Chris."

Hunter stands quickly, sending his seat crashing backward on the floor.

"*She's* the chosen one?"

The rest of the pack stands, ready for battle.

I eyeball Hunter, and he growls at me.

"Don't," I say, but I already know it's gone too far.

"I would rather die than let her fall into your arms, Liberator."

I glance at the elf. "Trust me." "Never,"

Chris replies.

I smile, my fangs extend, I upend the table, shove the elf, scoop up Angelica, and flee into the night. I know I have to dampen her scent for the lycans and elf will be able to follow us. The only place I can think to go to is Central Park, so I increase my speed.

"Holy fuck!"

"You're safe," I whisper.

"Why did you run?" Angelica sounds scared, and I know running at these speeds can be frightening to humans.

"Close your eyes and take a deep breath."

"Why? What?"

I run into the middle of the lake in Central Park. When I stop moving, we plunge into its depths. Angelica struggles against me, but I hold her fast.

When we hit the bottom, I run. I can feel her fists striking me as she tries to get loose. When we get to the other side and out of the water, Angelica takes a deep breath, choking as she expels water. She continues to strike me, but I keep going until I have her inside my apartment, door locked, and her standing in the bathroom.

"W-what the actual fuck!" screeches Angelica.

I step back from her, and she stumbles, landing on her butt.

I kneel in front of her, hands raised. "It was necessary to keep you safe. If you're the chosen one, the pack would have wanted you for themselves. I can't imagine you'd want Hunter by your side for all time."

"You're all insane!" Angelica gets to her feet—some weed is hanging off the end of her ponytail.

Slowly, so as not to alarm her, I stand. "Shower. Get clean. I'll not disturb you."

"What? Are you crazy? I'm outta here, buddy." My fangs extend, and I step into her space.

She immediately backs up, hands in front of her. "I'll not harm you. I will take you to the witches. You need to trust me."

Angelica's eyes are wide with fear, and it makes my jaw ache. She is young, innocent, and her fear makes my predatory side yearn for her.

I hold out my hand and touch her beautiful face, and the electricity sizzles up my arm. My cock becomes hard, and I press myself against her, running my fangs up her neck. Angelica shivers and whimpers. The urge to bite and drink her is overwhelming.

"P-please."

The tone of her voice gets through to me, and I lean back. Angelica is terrified. With a growl, I move back.

"Shower," I command as I force myself to leave the room.

CHAPTER EIGHT

Angelica

Janardan leaves the bathroom so fast, I fall to my knees. I've never been so scared in my life. With his fangs extended and his strength up against me, I have no idea why he didn't end me. I crawl to the door and lock it.

"Do you really think I can't break the door down? Shower, Angelica, or I'm coming in there to help you."

There's a roughness to his voice, sounding almost feral. Quickly, I stand and turn the shower on. The water is cold, and as the spray hits me, I yelp.

"Are you all right?" Janardan's voice is filled with concern.

"I'm fine," I yell out quickly.

I turn the hot water on and stand there, not knowing what to do.

"Angelica, throw your clothes out so I can wash them. Take your time. I will *not* harm you."

"Yeah, right," I mutter to myself as I struggle to get out of my boots and clothing.

"I swear to you. I'll not do anything to you that you don't want me to do."

Damn vampire hearing.

"Yeah, well, you can probably glamour me and make me do anything," I say hysterically.

"Vampires do *not* glamour people. That's strictly nonsense, something for teenage girls on TV. I'd be more than happy to teach you the ways of the vampire."

"I'm good."

When I'm free of my clothing, I step out of the shower, open the door as much as I need to and let them fall on the floor in a watery heap. I'm mentally hoping they ruin his floors, then I lock the door and go back into the shower. Something green hits the floor of the shower, and I scream.

The door instantly bursts open, and Janardan is staring at me, fangs extended looking like he wants to eat me. To protect my dignity, I turn around and face the shower wall.

"What?" he demands to know.

"There's something green in the shower."

Janardan laughs, and like before, it does something to me. It's an almost magical sound. It doesn't make sense that this man can affect me so. I should be trying to escape, but I find myself listening to him.

"It's from the lake. It's just a weed that's gotten caught in your hair," he whispers.

"Umm, good. Could you go now?"

Janardan places a hand on either side of my head, and his chest touches my back. I don't feel any clothing and press myself into the shower wall to get away from him.

"Don't fear me."

"Ahh... are you naked?"

His lips touch my shoulder. "Yes."

Electricity runs through me from my shoulder to my pussy. Janardan breathes deeply.

"Do you like that?"

"No. What I'd like is for you to leave," I lie.

I feel his hand as it travels from my waist to my breast, and the feeling is more sensual than anything I've experienced before. My knees buckle, and his other arm swiftly goes around me, pinning me to him. I can feel his erection against my back. Janardan's lips travel from my shoulder to my ear, and I feel his fangs as they scrape against my neck.

"P-please."

"Please?"

I don't understand what's happening to me. Part of me wants him to keep going, but I've only just met him, and let's face it, he's scary.

"Please leave."

Janardan tenses. "You want me to leave?" I

nod, fearing my voice will betray me.

His hands rest on my hips, and his body moves away from mine. "Forgive me," he whispers.

"It's okay. If you leave now, it'll be okay."

"That's not what I want you to forgive me for."

One of his arms snakes its way up my body between my breasts, crushing me against him, and his mouth comes down on my neck. At first, he sucks there, and then I feel the sting of his fangs as they pierce my flesh.

"No!" I cry out, but the pain quickly turns to pleasure, and my body betrays me as my need takes over. I arch against him, wantonly. With each pull on my neck, I can feel the pressure building

between my thighs. I open my l egs, and his other hand goes to my pussy but it's not enough. I need more.

I don't know whether it's the bite or the electric shock that is coursing through my body at his touch, but I have this staggering need to have him inside me.

"Stop!" I plead.

With a groan, Janardan retracts his fangs and releases me. I turn quickly and kiss him, walking him backward until he hits the far wall of the bathroom. I taste my own blood, and instead of it repulsing me, it tastes sweet. Janardan picks me up, and I lock my legs around his waist. His tongue teases mine as it darts in and out. I'm lost in the kiss, but when he sits me on the vanity, and I feel his cock at my entrance, I break us apart to stare him in the eyes as I pull him into me. The pain is immediate, and we both cry out, but as he moves, it lessens. When he again drinks from me, the pleasure is undeniable.

My body is moving in time with his. With each pull on my neck and thrust of his cock, my body searches for its release. Janardan moves faster. He grips my waist as he pounds in and out of me, and when his cock hits me in the right spot I shatter and scream out his name. The orgasm keeps building. I can no longer move as he continues his assault on my body. I've never experienced anything like this before. The pleasure he's eliciting is mind-blowing. Janardan growls loudly, and I feel his body tense as he pumps his seed into me. The electric feeling intensifies, and another orgasm sweeps through my being. It feels like I'm going to explode, then as it winds down and as the aftershocks subside, I look into Janardan's eyes, and they are completely black, there's no white.

I gasp, he shakes his head, and they return to normal. I rest my arms on his shoulders, and he carries me into a room that has no windows, and in the center is a very large four-poster bed.

Reverently, he lays me down, pulling out of me at the same time. I gasp at the loss of him, but it's more, it's like I'm missing a piece of myself.

"Did you feel that?" I ask.

"Yes," he whispers.

"I've never felt anything like that before. Is it because you're a vampire?"

"No, I've never felt anything like that either. It's because of you."

"I'm not going to get sick now, am I? Or turn into a vampire?"

Janardan chuckles and lays down beside me, tucking me into his side.

"Why would you get sick? And there's more to turning someone than a bite."

"Good to know. It's just the angel, Tristan, tried to have sex with me, and because we didn't actually do the deed, I got sick."

I feel him tense beside me and go up on one elbow to stare at him. "Are you okay?"

"The thought of another touching you is..." Janardan frowns and purses his lips. "Well, he kind of did it through a dream." "Fucking angels," hisses Janardan.

He reaches up and crushes my face to his, kissing me. My body lights up again, and the electric pull between us intensifies. I sit up and straddle him but don't take him into me. I grind on him, enjoying the feel of his cock as it gradually becomes harder.

"Why didn't you have sex with the angel?"

I stop what I'm doing and lock eyes with him. "It didn't feel like this. It felt good but not like this."

Janardan frowns and narrows his gaze. "I don't want to talk about him anymore."

"He kept asking if I'd give him permission to have my body."

"You didn't consent?"

I shake my head.

Janardan flips us, so he's on top. "Why did you let me?"

I break eye contact and look down the length of his body. He's all muscle and smooth skin.

"Angelica?"

I meet his eyes. "It felt overwhelming. It felt right." As I say this, a blush infuses my face. I know nothing about this man, and he kidnapped me. What the hell am I doing?

Janardan kisses me and moves down my throat, then to my nipples. His tongue flicks over them, making them pebble. I arch into him, and he chuckles. I feel the sting of his fangs as he drags them over my hip but doesn't draw blood. Janardan sucks on the inside of my thigh, and I open my legs for him. His eyes meet mine, and he smiles as he licks my slit. The current from his touch goes from my pussy to my nipples, and I cry out.

"Can I have your body?" he asks.

"Yes. You can have my body. Take me now!"

His cock rests at my entrance for a moment as he looks down at me. Janardan smiles, then rams into me. The orgasm hits me instantly, but it's different from before. I feel my body stretch and something within feels like it's snapping. Janardan cries out, his eyes wide as he too must feel this sensation. His fingers link with mine as he moves in and out. A red glow emanates between us, and as my orgasm reaches its peak, the light becomes so bright, it's blinding.

An electric shock goes between us, and then I'm falling.

Everything goes black, and I feel safe and cocooned with Janardan inside me.

CHAPTER NINE

Janardan

I wake up, and I'm lying half on Angelica, half on the bed. Her face is peaceful, and there's a small smile on her lips. Carefully, I move off her, and Angelica stirs but does not wake. The clock on my bedside table says eight fifteen. I look out my bedroom door, and sunlight bathes my apartment.

I look back at Angelica, and guilt washes over me. I haven't tasted innocent blood in a very long time. I close my eyes and center myself, and I don't feel any different. The blood of an innocent normally gives you a feeling of euphoria like a drug you have to have more. I lean down and inhale her scent, my fangs don't extend, and my jaw doesn't ache. I kiss her lightly on the forehead and walk out into my apartment, pulling on pants as I go.

My phone is on the kitchen bench. I pick it up and move toward the windows to look out over the park. The sun warms me, and I realize I'm not burning. I'm standing in full sunlight, and I'm fine. I stare up into the sun's rays and feel them warm my face. It's been so long, I had forgotten how good it can feel.

I scroll through my phone until I find Levi, the head of my clutch's phone number. I hit dial and wait as it seems to ring for a long time.

"This is the phone of the sire of the clutch, state your business," says a woman in a bored tone.

"Hello, I'm Janardan, is Levi available?"

"Our sire is most busy and does not take calls unless you have an appointment."

The line goes dead. I stare at the screen and realize she's hung up on me. I hit redial.

"Don't hang up on me. Tell Levi who's on the phone, and he will take my call. My name is Janardan."

I hear her shallow breathing and then hold music blares into my ear.

Abruptly, it stops, and she says, "Putting you through now, sir."

She sounds contrite, and frankly, I don't care. I will find out who she is later.

"What do you want, Jan, it's early," says Levi.

"Your secretary hung up on me. I'm not amused."

"Did you say who you were?"

"Well, of course, I did," I let out a growl. "Levi, I only called you to get Abigail's phone number." "She's no longer High Priestess. It's Evie." "I'm aware of that," I reply impatiently.

"Why do you want to speak with a witch?"

"Levi, can you just give me the number?" I frown and let out a sigh. I do not want to tell him that the vampire race may be in a position of power. He already has far too much of it as sire of the clutch.

"You missing your old flame? I have to tell you she doesn't look like she once did," Levi chuckles.

"I know."

"You know? Why? Have you been in contact with the witches? Is it because of the prophecy?" Levi's tone is urgent and demanding.

"Yes, it was because of their stupid prophecy," I say in a bored tone so as not to spark his interest.

"What did they say?"

"Levi, you know what they said. The same thing they always say. The chosen one is among us. Something, I might add, that *you* should have forewarned me about."

Levi chuckles. "Did you kill anyone?"

"No," I laugh. "Although Evie could do with a good bleeding."

The sound of Levi's laughter filters down the line. "Yes, yes, she could. Very intense, that one. Why do you want Abigail's number?"

"She's not well. I left her some of my blood, and I want to make sure she has enough." A truth mixed in with a lie. Hopefully, he can't tell.

"Old age is a bitch. Fine, I'll text it to you." I can hear him breathing on the other end.

"Is there something else, Levi?"

"Do you think they've found her?"

"The chosen one? No, the witches haven't found her." To try and divert his attention, I ask, "What would you do if you found her?"

"Claim her. As a race, we would become unstoppable."

I laugh as I look down on the humans walking along the streets.

"It's all about power for you, isn't it?"

"Is there anything else?"

"Sleep well, Levi, and don't forget to text me."

I hang up and stare at the brightness of the day. I had forgotten how beautiful everything looks in the sun.

Angelica comes up behind me. I can hear her quiet footsteps. She wraps her arms around me and rests her head on my back.

"Are you all right?" I ask.

"Mmm… I feel wonderful. But I am hungry."

I twist in her arms and place mine around her. "I have food. What would you like?"

"A grilled cheese?"

I laugh and walk her toward the kitchen.

"Your wish is my command."

"So, all the things about vampires aren't true?"

"What do you mean, angel?"

"Angel? Hmm… I think I like the way you say that." I smile and get a block of cheese out of the fridge. "You know they don't eat, you can't walk in the sun, and all that. Can you eat garlic?"

I chuckle and begin to slice the cheese. "I haven't walked in the sun for over a thousand years. Yes, we eat. Not a lot of garlic as it makes digesting blood harder, something to do with an enzyme. It's an unpleasant feeling."

"Wait, you haven't been in the sun for a thousand years? But you were just at the window."

"I think it's you, angel. Your blood, and the fact you let me claim you. It's the only thing I can think of."

"So, I'm like a superhuman?"

I chuckle. "It would seem you are the chosen one."

"What does that mean exactly?" Angelica's brow is furrowed, and she chews on her bottom lip.

"It's prophesied that you will unite the races."

"How many races are there?"

"I will answer any of your questions, but I believe we need to take you to the Council of Witches. And to the best of my knowledge, there are eight races."

Angelica tilts her head to the side, and I hand her a slice of cheese. She nibbles on it and looks thoughtful. "Why did you say to the best of your knowledge?"

"Some races are believed to have died out and have not been seen for a long time, but there are some that believe they are waiting in the shadows for you."

"What makes me so special?"

I continue to make her a grilled cheese as I answer.

"Who were your parents?"

Angelica shakes her head. "I don't know. I grew up in foster homes."

I hit the coffee machine and grab two cups out of the cupboard. "That must have been hard." I take in what she's wearing and realize it's one of my dress shirts. "Nice shirt."

Angelica blushes and looks coy. "I hope you don't mind, I couldn't find my clothes."

"Oh shit," I mutter as I walk to the main bathroom. Sure enough, her clothes are still in the damp pile we left them in.

I pick them up and take them into the laundry room. When I return to Angelica, she's made us both a coffee and is eating her grilled cheese.

"This is good." Angelica smiles widely at me.

"I'm glad." I take one of her hands and bring it to my lips, the need to touch her is unsettling. Angelica links her fingers with mine and sighs. "Do you feel it, too?"

"Yes, I feel so much better touching you."

Reluctantly, I let her go and drop to my knees.

"Janardan, what are you doing?"

Looking at the floor, I say, "I'm so sorry. I'll never again put my needs before yours. You will *always* come first..." I pause, searching for the right words to say. "What I did to you last night can't be forgiven. I only ask that you trust me enough to know I will defend you with my life."

Angelica's hands touch my face, and she slides

off the chair and onto the floor in front of me. "Nothing that you did last night was bad. It all felt amazing. Even you feeding off me was..." Angelica shakes her head. "The only word I can think of is amazing. But, it was so much more than that. Janardan, I wanted you last night as much as you wanted me."

I meet her eyes, and I know she's talking the truth. Leaning in, I kiss her lightly on the lips.

"We need to get you to the witches. Best we do it today. Now. After you've had enough to eat, of course."

"And clean clothes?"

I chuckle as she throws her arms around my neck. "Yes, and clean clothes."

CHAPTER TEN

Janardan

With her hand firmly entwined with mine, we make our way through the streets of New York City. I take her down the alley that Baracus took me down, except it feels like a million years ago. I told Abigail that I had no intention of being mated, and now I can't imagine my life without Angelica. My every thought is to take care of her and make sure she is protected.

When we get to the end of the alley, I look at Angelica's beautiful face and stop our progression.

"Don't let the witches confuse you or believe anything they tell you about me. If you have questions, I promise I'll answer them, but perhaps not here. Can you do that?"

"This is going to sound totally insane, but somehow, I know you're telling me the truth." Angelica holds up our hands. "Tell me a lie." "What?"

"Tell me a lie," repeats Angelica.

"You're the ugliest woman I've ever laid eyes on."

Angelica gasps. "Way harsh! But I *know* you're lying, it's so weird."

I chuckle and pull her into me. "Ready?"

"Yep. Let's do this."

I open the door, turn left, and find the trap door. I open it, and Angelica peers inside.

"Where does it lead?"

"To the witches' coven. Don't break our bond," I say, holding up our hands.

"Okay. How do we do this? Do we climb down?"

I raise my eyebrows, pull her into me, and say, "Do you trust me?"

"With my life."

I smirk at her, tighten my grasp, and fall into the open trapdoor. Angelica screams, and after ten seconds, she stops.

"What the fuck?"

"The witches way of checking us out. It's a spell. We feel like we're falling but in actuality, we're about a foot off the floor. They are checking us out, seeing what we are made of."

"It's weird."

I chuckle. I keep her hand in mine but let her go. "Does it not feel like we're flying?"

Angelica gives me a half-smile and looks at me sideways. "Yes, it's kind of cool."

Suddenly, we hit the floor. I move quickly to make sure Angelica does not fall over.

"Liberator, I see you've come to visit us again?" says Evie as she looks at us quizzically.

"Evie," I reply curtly. "Are your witches watching us?"

"Of course."

"Ask them what they see."

Evie motions for us to follow her, the floor lights up as she navigates through the dark hallways of her coven.

"How did you get here through the day, Janardan?" asks Evie.

"We walked," replies Angelica.

Evie laughs. "Fine, don't tell me. Abigail and some of the others are in the library. Perhaps you will answer all our questions then."

"We really did walk. It's a beautiful day."

Evie smiles at me, shakes her head, and continues. She does not ask us another question until we enter the library with Abigail, Gloria, and Patricia.

"Why are you here, Janardan?" demands Evie.

"Evie, this is Angelica. I believe her to be the chosen one."

Evie looks at the other witches who say nothing, but all appear to be staring at us avidly.

"Their auras are white," says Abigail as she shakes her head. "What do you see?" asks Abigail to Gloria and Patricia.

In unison, they say, "White."

"Well, there you go. She can't be the chosen one, it should be red."

"Unless he's claimed her. If he's done that, then their auras could change," replies Abigail.

Angelica looks up at me. "Maybe I'm not what everyone thinks I am."

"Who else thinks you're the chosen one?" asks Evie as she pours herself a drink.

"Chris, he's an elf and the king's son."

"Eruaphadion?" asks Evie skeptically.

"I only know him as Chris. He says it's the English translation of his real name."

"She speaks the truth, Evie, that's his English name." Abigail stands and walks toward Angelica, holding out her hands. "Grab hold, child, and let's see what you are."

Angelica looks up at me, and I nod, releasing her hand. Hesitantly, Angelica puts her hands in Abigail's.

Abigail gasps and stares at Evie. "Oh, no! There's still so much to teach you. I'm sorry, my sweet girl, trust in yourself. Trust Jan. I'll always be with you." Angelica screams and tries to let go of Abigail. There's a blinding flash, and before my eyes, Abigail begins to turn to dust.

"Take care of her Jan, she's the one," whispers Abigail before she disintegrates.

Cardinal

Angelica screams and throws herself at me. Evie drops to her knees at what is left of her grandmother on the carpet, and the other two begin to chant. The ring on my finger burns and I double over in pain.

Angelica drops to her knees in front of me. "Janardan, what's wrong?"

I hold up my hand, and the ring is glowing, it looks white-hot. Without hesitation, Angelica grabs the ring and wrenches it off my finger. As soon as it is no longer on me, I feel normal and hiss at the witches, both of whom back away from me.

"Why didn't you just take it off? It came off easily," says Angelica.

"I couldn't. Only the chosen one can remove it." I glare at the witches who were chanting, and they've gone quiet, fear in their eyes.

Evie has her hands in the dust that was once Abigail and is silently crying.

"What just happened?" asks Angelica.

Evie looks up at Angelica. "*You* are what happened."

I put myself between the two women, keeping Angelica's hand firmly within my grip and stare down at Evie's tear-stained face.

"We didn't know this would happen. I thought you said it would be a month before Abigail left."

Evie stares at me nodding, unable to speak

"It's because they touched. Abigail must have felt it as soon as they held hands," says Gloria. "Oh, Evie, I'm so sorry."

Evie stands as fresh tears flow. I hold out my hand to steady her, and as she puts her hand in mine, a jolt goes through my system, and I find myself stretched up and levitating off the floor. I look to my right, and Angelica is also off the floor, arched back, eyes rolled back in her head. Gloria and Patricia are in front of me, shock across their faces. Both fall to their knees, holding hands looking desperately at us.

"Do something," I hiss.

"We can't. It's up to you three. The energy in this room is almost suffocating. You need to ground them, Janardan, and do it now!"

Not knowing what they mean, I try to break the connection with Evie but am not able to do so. It's like my muscles have a mind of their own. I pull Angelica closer, and her hand strikes out and grabs Evie. There's a bright flash of light, and we all hit the floor hard. Evie falls on her ass, but I manage to keep Angelica and me upright.

"Janardan?" whispers Angelica, fear lacing her tone.

"It's okay, it's okay, You're safe." I pull her into my arms and move away from the witches.

Evie stands, and she's staring at her hands. A smile creeps across her face, and she looks to her companions. "She's the chosen one. I feel Abigail's magic within me, and I can feel Angelica's power from here. Do you feel it?"

Both the witches nod, and all stare at us. I protectively move Angelica away from them.

"What just happened?" I demand to know.

Evie ignores me and moves around the room, trying to get a better look at Angelica.

"Don't come any closer, or *I will* end you."

Evie shakes her head. "I mean her no harm. Angelica, how do you feel?"

Angelica looks up at me. "I feel like I've been zapped with energy like I could run a marathon, but at the same time, my mind feels as though it's had a download of information, and it's hard to think straight."

I watch Evie carefully. She's nodding, and her smile turns into a grin. She's circling us, and I don't like it. Angelica looks at Evie and screams. I snarl at the witches and move Angelica further away from them.

"What is it?" I ask.

"Their faces! Can you not see their faces?"

I stare at the witches and slowly move my mate further away from them. I don't know what Angelica is seeing, but I know she's terrified.

Evie holds up her hands. "Angelica, it's not our faces you're seeing but our auras. Calm down, close your eyes, take a deep breath, and then try to look at us again."

Angelica is shaking. I press my lips to her temple trying to calm her. "Do it, angel, I promise they won't hurt you."

With a shuddering breath, she does as she's told.

Evie takes a step toward us, and I hold up a finger, my fangs extend, and she quickly retreats.

"Angel, I want you to look at me first, and together we'll face the witches. Okay?" She nods and slowly opens her eyes. "How do I look?"

"Handsome, sexy, and... mine."

I grin down at her, and she gives me a small smile. "Good answer. Take a deep breath and then look at the others."

Angelica does as she is told. Her body goes rigid in my arms, and she shakes her head from side to side.

"What is it?" I ask.

"They have writing all over them. Some of the words look like they are pulsing. Can't you see it?"

I close my eyes, center myself, take a deep breath, and focus on Evie. The façade she projects to the world melts away, and I can see what Angelica sees. She no longer looks nice. There's a sinister air to her now.

"What do you see?" asks Evie.

"Exactly what Angelica sees. There are words and symbols all over you. And you appear to be in muted tones like the light has seeped out of you." Evie smiles and claps her hands. She turns to the other two, and they all embrace.

"She really is the chosen one, isn't she?" asks Gloria.

"Indeed. And she's in *our* coven," exclaims Evie.

I do not like where this conversation is heading and begin to move Angelica toward the door.

With her back to me, Evie says, "Not so fast, Janardan. She might be your mate, but she's in our coven. We'll not let you take her from us."

"Evie, we came to you for answers, but I'll not allow you to hurt Angelica. She's mine to protect."

"Yes, the powers that be have definitely picked well when they chose you for her mate." Evie moves away from us and pours herself a drink. "But Angelica is too valuable. We can't let her go. Surrender her to us, and we won't kill you."

"You think I'm that easy to kill?"

The witches all cackle between themselves and nod.

"You might be old, Liberator, but you aren't immortal. You can be killed and easily." Evie holds her hands up, chants something, and gives me an evil grin.

A flash of light streaks across the room and hits me in the chest. It warms me but does not hurt. I snarl at Evie, pick Angelica up, and sprint for the way out.

"No," yells Evie.

I keep going, and when I find the trap door, I jump up and out into the alley and keep running until I am miles away from them.

I look down at Angelica, and she has her eyes closed.

"Are you okay?" I ask.

"How fast can you run?"

I chuckle. "Faster than you." I put her on her feet, and she looks around. "Angel, I don't know what to do," I admit.

"Chris will know."

"The elf? I don't know," I say as I shake my head.

"He's my friend."

"I thought the witches would be on our side, but the power you hold within you is clearly too much for any one race."

"I don't feel that different. Except—"

"What?"

"I don't know, it's like I can hear voices in my head. Maybe I'm going crazy?"

"What are the voices saying?"

Angelica shakes her head. "They're all talking too quickly, and at once. They overlap. I can't make out anyone in particular."

"Ring your friend. Ask to meet in Central Park where he took you for the cleansing."

"The cleansing?"

"Yes, angel, the place you woke up naked and sticky."

"How do you know about that?"

"Vampire senses," I reply, tapping my nose.

"Eww!" Angelica gets her cell phone out and hits some buttons and puts it to her ear. "Hello, Chris," she says, and a smile lights up her face.

I can't help it. I snarl, and my fangs extend. I don't like her being happy at the sound of the elf's voice.

"I'm fine! No, really..." Angelica pauses as she listens to him. "Janardan wants us to meet in Central Park where you cleansed me." She nods her head and smiles at me. "No, now." Angelica shakes her head. "Let us worry about the daylight. See you in thirty minutes?" She nods again and says, "Bye."

Grinning at me, she puts the phone back in her pocket and looks up at me.

"I don't like the elf."

"*Chris* is a good guy."

"The elf may have told the troupe about you by now. We should get to the park first to see if he's sent anyone ahead to ambush us."

"Chris wouldn't do that."

"I didn't think the witches would try and take you from me, but they did. We need answers, and I'm not sure who to trust."

Angelica goes up on her tiptoes and kisses me. As she tries to pull away, I cup the back of her head and deepen the kiss. My tongue plays with hers, and she moans into my mouth.

"Keep making noises like that, and I'll take you here."

Angelica looks around at the buildings and people. "There's nowhere private."

I pick her up and run to the top of a building. There's no one around and begin to kiss her while my hands roam her body.

"Janardan, where are we?"

"Private," I state as I kiss her neck.

"We look so high up."

I cup her face in my hands and look her in the eyes. "We only have thirty minutes, angel. Let's make the most of it."

My fangs extend, and I suckle and kiss her neck as my hands tease her body. When Angelica moans, I plunge my fangs into her, then undo her belt and jeans, and I touch her most sensitive parts. With each pull, she grinds against my hand, urging me on.

I feel her pussy contract around my fingers as I continue to drink from her. Angelica cries out, and when I draw out every last aftershock from her, I lick closed my mark and put my forehead to hers.

"That can't have been very good for you," whispers my angel.

"I know it's hard to comprehend, but I feel what you feel when I'm feeding. It's not as good as burying my cock inside you, but it's a damn close second."

My angel smiles at me. "Your turn next time."

"Agreed."

"We should go."

I give her a nod and grab her around the waist. "Hold on."

With a wicked grin, Angelica kisses me. "I always do."

I chuckle and begin to run to our destination.

CHApTER ELEVEN

Angelica

The speed with which Janardan maneuvers through the city is terrifying. I close my eyes for most of it. I've never felt so loved or cared for. It's like we fast-forwarded through all the awkward stages of our relationship and have gone straight into the love stage. In the space of a day, I can't imagine my life without him. And deep down, I know Janardan feels the same way too. I feel unsettled if we aren't touching, and when we do touch, my nerve endings want more. So much more.

"Angel, you can open your eyes now," says Janardan in a soothing tone.

I crack open one eye and see we are at the place I woke up with Chris leaning over me. That all feels like so long ago.

Opening both eyes, I take a step away from Janardan but keep his hand firmly held in mine. "Is Chris here?"

Janardan smiles and looks around, nodding. "Yes, and he's not alone." "Chris,"

I yell.

In his projected image, Chris steps from behind a tree. I smile and wave at him as he approaches, giving Janardan a wide berth.

"Hello, Ange. Word has spread quickly that the chosen one is among us, and the troupe sent more of my kind to," Chris pauses as he seems to be searching for the right words. "Welcome you." "Why do you look like the old you?" I ask.

Chris frowns and looks down. "Habit." He closes his eyes and morphs into his true self. "Better?"

"I'm not sure. But if this is the real you, then you should always present yourself so. I want you to be comfortable."

Chris grins, and when he gets close to me, he wraps me in a hug. It's not easy as Janardan does not release my hand.

"I'm so glad you're okay, Ange."

I pull back from him, grinning. "Why wouldn't I be okay?"

Janardan pulls me back against his body. I glance up at him and notice he's scanning the area around us.

"Chris, tell your friends to come out. They're making Janardan nervous."

Chris laughs mirthlessly. "They're making *him* feel nervous? Do you have any idea who he is? What he's done? He's as close to a monster as you'll get."

His words hurt me, and I shake my head. "No. *I know him*, Chris. I can't explain it, but I know his deepest darkest secrets, and he doesn't scare me. Janardan isn't the same man anymore."

Chris shakes his head, raises his hand, and five elves move out into plain view. I feel Janardan relax beside me a fraction. Chris looks over me to Janardan.

"You've claimed her, haven't you?"

"Yes. It wasn't planned. I couldn't control myself." At Janardan's words, Chris' face turns red.

"I swear I didn't hurt her."

"It shouldn't have been you," yells Chris.

I move out of Janardan's arms to grab Chris' hands, and he immediately calms down.

"It shouldn't have been him," whispers Chris.

"But it was. Is. I feel like I've found another part of me that I didn't know was missing. But I have so many questions, Chris. The witches were of no help. They were going to kill him and use me for their own devices. Chris, can you help me? Us?"

Chris' face softens. The other elves make no move to come closer.

"Truth," says Chris.

I nod. "Truth."

Chris lets out a shuddering breath. "The troupe can help. Now that you've been claimed, it will make it harder. The clutch will lay claim to you."

"No," says Janardan forcefully. "I'm a rogue vampire. I've never pledged to Levi and the clutch."

Chris draws his eyebrows together, then smiles, smoothing out his frown. "So, she didn't pick a race, Ange picked you. This is good. This is very good."

"Why is it good?" I ask, completely confused.

"For the prophecy is coming true." Chris puts his forehead to mine. "Come with me to meet our king. He will answer any of your questions, truthfully."

I look over my shoulder to Janardan. He places a hand on my shoulder and drags me back into his frame.

"Chris is right, the elvin king will hold many answers."

"I still don't like you," states Chris.

"He'll grow on you," I reply.

"Like a fungus?"

Janardan growls, but I giggle.

"Don't tease him. Janardan's patience isn't infinite. Lead the way."

Chris smirks and moves out into the open ground, the other elves draw in around him. All bar one elf avoids eye contact with me. The one who is brave enough to meet my gaze quickly looks away. I look up at Janardan quizzically, and he shrugs, shaking his head slightly.

"Give me your hand, Ange."

"I'm coming with her," states Janardan.

Chris looks thoughtful. "Okay. We've never had one of your kind in our city before. I don't know how the royal guard is going to handle this. Stay close to Angelica and pray they don't shoot you."

"Charming," replies Janardan sarcastically.

Chris holds out a hand to him. "Okay, let's get this show on the road."

Janardan kisses me on the temple, and grasps Chris' and my hand.

"You okay?" I ask.

Janardan gives me a small smile. "So long as we do this together, I'll be okay."

"Oh, enough already. Clear your minds," says Chris tersely.

The other elves move in, encircling us. The air around us shimmers, and the ground we are standing on vibrates, then I feel like I'm falling. It all takes a blink of an eye, and then I'm in the most beautiful garden I have ever seen. All the colors around me appear brighter, and the fragrance that invades my senses is potent.

"Prince Eruaphadion, why have you brought this abomination into my realm?" booms a man clad in armor with his sword drawn.

Chris moves in front of Janardan, and I place an arm around his waist.

"Apologies, Captain Woodland. He's the mate of the chosen one, and neither would come without the other."

"That does not explain how he's able to stand here in broad daylight. He should be nothing but ashes."

Captain Woodland advances toward us, and I drag Janardan back.

"Captain! Stand down!" yells Chris as he turns to face us. "How the hell are you able to be out in broad daylight? I can't believe I didn't notice that until now." Chris looks annoyed with himself.

I only have eyes for Captain Woodland, who is moving past Chris, eyes glued to Janardan.

Janardan drops down to one knee. "I'm hers, and she's mine. I'll not hurt her or anyone here for as long as Angelica draws a breath."

"See, Captain… he's given his word."

"The word of the Liberator does not hold much value," sneers Captain Woodland.

"Okay, buddy, you're going to have to go through me if you want to hurt Janardan. I'm not as fragile as I look."

I assume a fighter's pose, and Captain Woodland and Chris both stare at me with disbelief, then Chris, the bastard, begins to laugh. Captain Woodland cocks his head and looks from Chris to me.

"You both protect this vile creature?"

"Seriously, if you call him names one more time, I'm going to bitch slap you."

Chris buckles over, clutching his stomach, laughing with tears streaming down his face. Captain Woodland looks perplexed and slowly lowers his sword.

"Hmm, my son finally returns home with a vampire and a human," says a man in a very bored tone.

"Father," exclaims Chris as he grips the man's forearm in the form of a handshake, arm shake.

"Eruaphadion, why are they here?"

"Aran, it's good to see you." Chris turns and sweeps his arm toward me. "This is Angelica Adam, the chosen one. And unfortunately, her mate, Janardan."

"*The* Janardan?" asks the king in a slightly interested tone.

"Yes, my lord, the very same."

"Hmm, this is disconcerting." The king waves Captain Woodland off. "Enough, Captain. Come, Angelica, Janardan, walk with me so we might sort out this mess."

Aran tilts his head directing us where to go and walks away with Chris right beside him. I let out a breath I didn't realize I was holding.

"Are you okay, angel?"

"That was all very intense. Are you okay?"

Janardan stands, brushing off his pants as he does. "We should catch up before the captain decides to end me."

I glance over at the captain, and although he has put his sword away, he appears to be pondering Janardan's words. I grab Janardan's hand and drag him toward Aran and Chris. When we catch up to them, Chris glances at me and smiles. I return it with one of my own. Aran sits at a long table and gestures for us to sit as well. I look over at Captain Woodland, but he doesn't join us. Instead, he positions himself behind the elvin king.

"Are you sure she's the one?" asks Aran.

Chris nods and looks at me mischievously. "Yes, my lord… on her twenty-fifth birthday, her powers came into effect. Unfortunately, I missed the beginning."

"Why did you not bring her to me immediately?"

"There was an incident with the angel, Tristan."

"Incident?"

I feel my face burning red, and Janardan lets off a low growl.

"We don't really need to talk about that right now. Let's just say the angel poisoned me."

Aran chuckles and raises his eyebrows. "I see. So, the angels thought to claim you, but it seems the vampire beat them. Interesting." Aran has one arm bent and tapping his lips with his hand, studying me, then he turns his blue gaze to Janardan. "And you... how do you have a white aura? And how is it possible for you to be in the sunlight?"

"I believe it's Angelica. I feel connected to her like no other, and her blood is like nectar."

"You've fed off her? The chosen one? How is it your eyes aren't black and the taint of the crave isn't upon you?"

Janardan shakes his head and reaches for my hand under the table.

"I don't know. I believe it's because she's the chosen one that all this is possible."

Aran slams his hand hard on the table causing me to jump.

"Fear not, little one, this is all mystifying." Aran turns his gaze to Chris. "Go fetch the tomes on the chosen one."

"There are tomes?" asks Janardan.

"Yes, of course. We kept them from the other races. We have suspected many to be the chosen one over the centuries. You're the one closest to the written word so far." Aran's eyes flick to Janardan.

"And the fact that the vampire is in the sun and not afflicted by feeding on you would suggest that all this is true, but I'd still like to consult the written word."

"So, there's been others like me?"

"No," replies Chris immediately. "None have been able to do what you can do."

"But what have I been able to do?"

Chris smiles. "You see me in my true form, and I suspect there have been others besides the angel. And you had an elf, a lycan, and a vampire sit down at the same table. That hasn't happened in an age."

"That doesn't prove anything. We were all hungry," I say earnestly.

"No, Angelica, it was you. All I wanted was to be near you. The lycan and the vampire were both tracking you. Why do you think that was? And you and the vampire both saw red birds."

"His name is Janardan, stop calling him the vampire. It's not nice, Chris. How would you like it if I called you the elf all the time?"

Under the table, Janardan squeezes my hand a little tighter, and when I glance at him, he smiles.

"Angelica is right, Chris. You should call him by his name. Now, go fetch me the tomes," demands Aran.

"Why can't you say books? Tomes sounds very stuffy," I ask, which causes the elvin king to bark out a laugh.

"Yes, of course, go fetch the books, *Chris*."

"Yes, father, and you don't have to call me by my English name."

Aran smiles at him fondly. "I think she likes it. Now go!"

Chris stands and bows, then hurries away.

"Could I interest you in something to eat and drink?" asks Aran.

"Will it mean I can't leave here? Is it some sort of trick?" I ask.

Janardan laughs, but Aran looks shocked.

"Your highness, it's an old legend about the king or queen of the fae, not elves. I'm afraid Angelica has gotten the two confused." Janardan looks at me. "And it's not true of either race, my love. Neither would trick you nor do I think they'd be able to."

"Yes, indeed, if she is, in fact, the chosen one, none will be able to trick her in such a way," agrees Aran.

I have superpowers? Cool.

CHAPTER TWELVE

Angelica

Aran put the most scrumptious sandwiches and drinks in front of me that I have ever tasted. I ate twice as much as anyone else, and I'm still hungry. I look longingly at the empty platter, and the old king chuckles. He signals to someone behind me, and a fresh platter is placed in front of me.

"Where do you put it?" asks Janardan.

"I don't normally eat *this* much, but I'm famished."

"Perhaps it's the feedings?" asks Chris staring at Janardan.

"Perhaps? Although I don't know what she was like before we met."

Chris looks at me thoughtfully. "She did like sweet things."

"Hello, sitting right here. I've always eaten a lot, but this is weird even for me." I go to put the halfeaten sandwich down but decide against it. It would be wasteful.

"Well, Aran, what have you discovered?" asks Janardan as he refills my glass with water.

"The tomes... excuse me, *books*... say that Angelica will come into her powers one month after her twenty-fifth birthday. Until then, she's vulnerable. Her powers will slowly emerge and then come to an apex." Aran looks at me and smiles. "Your powers should enable you to bring peace and prosperity to all the races." "Should?" I ask.

"I'm unclear how that's supposed to happen," replies Aran as he closes the last of the books. "The humans have been blind to us for so long that I don't know how they'll react. My guess is badly."

"You know, we may not know you're here, but there have been myths, legends, and TV shows. In a way, we've known all about you for years." Chris spits his drink across the table.

"Angelica!"

"What?"

"Humans don't actually believe those things are real," states Chris.

"No, but what I'm saying is, we might not know for sure, but I think you'll be surprised at how well humans will handle the revelation that you aren't myth or legend."

"She has a point. Some of my..." I watch as Janardan tries to find the right words.

"Feeders?" I suggest.

Janardan's face goes slightly red, and he nods. "Yes, feeders. Some of them asked me to turn them into creatures of the night. That stupid movie ruined a lot of things."

"Twilight? That movie was great. The books were better. Did people want you to go into the sunlight and sparkle?"

"I don't sparkle," replies Janardan dryly.

"I know that, but it's what everyone will be thinking." I shake my head at him and grin.

"My angel, you have a strange way of looking at things."

I shrug my shoulders. "In a way, you've made my point. The people you fed off weren't that scared of you, were they?"

"In recent years, less and less." Janardan smiles creepily. "But in the end, they were scared."

"Eww! I can't believe you said that."

She settles, and I allow myself to relax and join her shortly after.

When I wake, the space where Angelica once laid is cold. I sit up and look around the room. She's not here. Breathing deeply, I follow her scent passing many guards whose hands tighten on their swords, but none draw them. I wind my way out of the palace and into the grounds where I come across Angelica with Chris laughing freely and trying to catch small balls of light.

"Janardan," squeals Angelica as she runs to me. "Faeries!" Angelica launches herself into my arms. "If you catch one, they grant a wish."

"That's not exactly true." I shake my head at Chris, who grins at me and shrugs.

"No, it is. You try."

I shake my head. "They are pixies, who will one day transform into the fae, and if you look at them now, they have banded together. They, like their older kin, fear me. I'll not be able to catch one unless they allow me to."

Angelica frowns and looks behind her. The pixies are all flying in a straight line. She releases me and moves toward them, and they fly away from her. Angelica looks heartbroken.

"He won't hurt you. I promise."

One of the pixies flies up to her face, and tentatively, Angelica raises her hand. The pixie lands on it.

"You're so brave," Angelica whispers.

I approach the pair of them.

Angelica turns, and the pixie lets out a screech and jumps onto her shoulder.

"She's right, little one. I'll not hurt you."

The pixie tilts its head to the side and flies within inches of my face. I smile at it, and it flies closer looking into my mouth.

"My fangs aren't visible at the moment. Would you like to see them?"

The pixie looks scared but nods. I let my fangs extend, and it screams, then I'm surrounded by all the pixies trying to get a better look.

I chuckle, and when I look over at Chris, he's doubled over in laughter, clutching his sides.

"What's so funny?" I ask.

"The pixies don't know what to make of you. Besides, if you try anything, there's enough of them to knock you unconscious for a week."

The little one that started all of this flies right up to one of my fangs and reaches out to touch it. I retract them, and it jumps back, laughing.

I bow my head to it. "On my life, I'll not hurt you."

Janardan grabs my hand and kisses the back of it. My insides melt at his touch, and I can't remember what I was talking about.

"Angelica?" asks Chris.

"Yes?" I look at him.

"Well, you can see that the mating ritual has completed itself," theorizes Chris.

I scowl at him as Janardan rubs my back trying to calm me down.

I swing my gaze back to Aran, who has a smile on his regal face.

"What's the plan?"

Aran leans forward. "Janardan needs to keep you safe. I know he's claimed you, but until the month is up, if another of the races mate with you, it could break your bond."

"Nope, not going to happen," I state.

Janardan growls low and deep, and I instinctively grab his hand.

"Angelica belongs to me, and I her."

Aran holds his hands up and slowly lowers them. "None in the troupe will challenge your claim. You and Angelica are safe here, but you can't stay here. We don't want another war with any of the races. Can you go to your clutch?"

"No. Levi would want to use Angelica to his own devices, and as I've never pledged myself to them. I fear I'd be disposable."

"You wouldn't be that easy to dispose of. You're the oldest and the most fearsome of your kind," says Chris.

"The witches?" asks Aran.

I shake my head. "No, they turned out to be not so nice."

"We know we can't trust the angels," states Chris.

"Where do I take her to keep her safe?"

Captain Woodland clears his throat. I'd forgotten he was even near us.

"Speak, captain," commands Aran.

"The herd, my Aran, they could protect her. I'm just not sure they would take the vampire into their fold."

"Their blood is intoxicating to my kind."

"But you have me now, right?" I ask Janardan earnestly.

"Yes, my angel, I have you." Janardan looks at Aran. "Make the request."

Aran nods and points to Captain Woodland. "Make it so."

Captain Woodland bows low and leaves us. I stifle a yawn, and Janardan looks at me closely.

"Aran, would it be possible for us to sleep for a while?"

"Of course." Aran stands. "Please follow me to the palace. Our beds are the most comfortable you will ever sleep in."

As one, the rest of us stand and follow the elvin king. I stumble a couple of times, so Janardan picks me up. With my head cradled against his chest, I feel myself drift off, and although it's not a bed, I am very comfortable.

CHApTER THIRTEEN

Janardan

I felt Angelica as she drifted off to sleep. She didn't even wake when I laid her down on the bed. Later, when I joined her, she stirred and rolled onto her side making it easy for me to pull her against my body, but still, she slept. I laid there for a long time listening to her breathing. The captain is correct, and the herd will not allow me into their borders. I am too much of a threat to them. In my younger days, I enjoyed hunting the imps, the bad fae. They are not common and cause much upheaval and mischief in the human world. I have never tasted a true faery, but I fear it would destroy me. Their smell alone is something to behold.

Angelica stirs, and I whisper to her, "Go to sleep, my angel, and dream of me."

She settles, and I allow myself to relax and join her shortly after.

When I wake, the space where Angelica once laid is cold. I sit up and look around the room. She's not here. Breathing deeply, I follow her scent passing many guards whose hands tighten on their swords, but none draw them. I wind my way out of the palace and into the grounds where I come across Angelica with Chris laughing freely and trying to catch small balls of light.

"Janardan," squeals Angelica as she runs to me. "Faeries!" Angelica launches herself into my arms. "If you catch one, they grant a wish."

"That's not exactly true." I shake my head at Chris, who grins at me and shrugs.

"No, it is. You try."

I shake my head. "They are pixies, who will one day transform into the fae, and if you look at them now, they have banded together. They, like their older kin, fear me. I'll not be able to catch one unless they allow me to."

Angelica frowns and looks behind her. The pixies are all flying in a straight line. She releases me and moves toward them, and they fly away from her. Angelica looks heartbroken.

"He won't hurt you. I promise."

Kathleen Kelly

One of the pixies flies up to her face, and tentatively, Angelica raises her hand. The pixie lands on it.

"You're so brave," Angelica whispers.

I approach the pair of them.

Angelica turns, and the pixie lets out a screech and jumps onto her shoulder.

"She's right, little one. I'll not hurt you."

The pixie tilts its head to the side and flies within inches of my face. I smile at it, and it flies closer looking into my mouth.

"My fangs aren't visible at the moment. Would you like to see them?"

The pixie looks scared but nods. I let my fangs extend, and it screams, then I'm surrounded by all the pixies trying to get a better look.

I chuckle, and when I look over at Chris, he's doubled over in laughter, clutching his sides.

"What's so funny?" I ask.

"The pixies don't know what to make of you. Besides, if you try anything, there's enough of them to knock you unconscious for a week."

The little one that started all of this flies right up to one of my fangs and reaches out to touch it. I retract them, and it jumps back, laughing.

I bow my head to it. "On my life, I'll not hurt you."

They all begin to wave and fly further into the garden.

"That was awesome," yells Angelica.

"Indeed," I agree.

Chris is still laughing, wiping tears away. "They'll be talking about you for a very long time." He looks at me and begins to nod. "You know this might work in your favor. If they tell the fae what you did, they might allow you entry into their city."

"I don't think the herd is that easily swayed."

Angelica puts her hand in mine. "If you don't go, I don't go."

"It will be safer for you there," I state.

"Don't care. This isn't up for debate. We're a team. If you don't go, I don't go," repeats Angelica more forcefully.

Chris shrugs. "She can be willful."

"I am not! If I were a man, we wouldn't even be having this conversation."

"You've got that right," I smirk.

Angelica's beautiful face breaks into a knowing grin. "You'd still love me."

"Yes, I'd still love you, but I wouldn't have sex with you."

"You love me?"

"That's all you heard?" I ask.

"You love me!"

"Yes, my angel, I love you.

Angelica does a small dance and then throws her arms around my neck. "I love you, too."

"I know."

"No, you didn't know 'cause I just told you."

I shake my head at her. "Some things don't need to be said, they can be felt."

"I prefer words."

Chris barks out a laugh and shakes his head. "Come on, chosen one, let's go eat, and then you can see if the herd will accept you both."

"Food. I'm hungry."

Angelica lets me go and follows Chris back toward the palace. The small pixie who was brave enough to approach me flies into my face.

"What is it, little one?"

The pixie appears to be holding something in its cupped hands. I lean in for a closer look. It smiles at me, draws back a hand, and throws what looks to be glitter into my face. I double over coughing and rub my eyes to get the substance out of them. When I can finally see and breathe normally again, I stand, and the little bastard is nowhere to be seen.

"I thought we were friends," I mutter to the garden then hurry to catch up with my mate.

Angelica looks heartbroken as she says goodbye to Chris and Aran. Both men embrace her lovingly and make her promise to come back. While Chris says his final goodbyes to Angelica, Aran takes me to one side.

"How did you do it?" "Do what?" I ask.

"How did you get the pixies to bless you?"

"What? One of the little brats threw grit in my face and flew away."

Aran chuckles. "It wasn't grit, it was a spell. A blessing spell saying you're a friend to the fae. Well done, Janardan. It may help you."

"He blessed me? I doubled over trying to breathe, and it stung my eyes."

"My guess is they were testing you. Had you not survived the blessing, say if your heart weren't pure, it probably would have killed you." "Killed me?" *Bloody pixies!* "Yes, but you survived." Angelica and Chris join us.

"Are you ready?" asks Chris.

"Yes," we both say.

Chris smiles. "Father, if you'd be so kind as to open a portal to the herd's homeland?"

Aran smiles and cups Angelica's face. "Be well and be safe, child. Trust your instincts, and all will be well."

A shimmering light envelops us, and one moment we are in the elvin kingdom, the next we are standing outside a grocery store in New York City.

"What the hell?" I ask.

"Oh, I think I know this place." Angelica turns around in a circle. "I think?"

"It's New York City, not the herd's homeland," I state.

"Did Aran make a mistake?"

"More likely the herd wouldn't allow me in, and we ended up here."

Angelica looks over my shoulder.

"There's chocolate in there."

I chuckle. "Would you like some chocolate?"

Nodding her head vigorously, Angelica grins at me and drags me into the store. A tall blond man sits behind the counter and straightens up as we enter. I smile at him, and his eyes bulge from his head.

"It's the middle of the day. And who the hell blessed you?" he asks completely frazzled.

Angelica smiles and walks right up to him and touches his hand, the man blinks at her and slowly transforms into one of the fae. He becomes taller, his hair longer, and has two long plaits either side of his face, but it's his eyes that show the most change. They become larger, more almond-shaped, and the brightest shade of blue you can imagine.

He flinches away from Angelica. "You again!"

"Again?" repeats Angelica, tilting her head to the side.

He's backed himself into the corner, eyes wild, looking for an escape.

"I'll not hurt you," I say as I take a few steps back.

"Vampires can't be trusted," he hisses.

With my hand on my chest, I bow slightly and say, "I'm Janardan, and this is Angelica. We were, in fact, searching for the herd. It appears we found you instead."

"Janardan? Liberator of the cycle of birth and death. Murderer!" screeches the fae.

"Perhaps once..." I pause and glance at Angelica, who's watching the man with unveiled interest, "... but to be fair, it was the great war, and there were deaths on both sides."

"You killed without remorse."

Angelica reaches out to touch him again, and he looks as though he's trying to melt himself into the wall.

"What's your name?" she asks.

The fae shakes his head violently from side to side.

"You said you'd met me before?"

"Yes. On the night of your becoming."

"Oh, you mean on my birthday? I met an angel, and he wiped most of my memories of that night. I'm sorry I don't remember you. So much has happened since then." As Angelica speaks, she inches closer to the fae, and she now has his hand in hers. "I've met demons, lycans, elves, and pixies. Have you met pixies? They are super cute." Angelica gestures toward me. "They're the ones who blessed Janardan. He's my mate, and he won't hurt you. I promise."

"Truth," sighs the fae.

Angelica nods and smiles. "Truth."

The fae slowly relaxes but does not move any closer toward me. He's hanging onto Angelica, and as he stares at her, he begins to glow and pulse.

"Wait," I yell.

Angelica immediately drops the fae's hand and moves closer to me.

"Is it not why you brought her to us so that we might protect her from you?"

"No, no, no," says Angelica quickly. "We're both seeking asylum with the herd. I can't part from Janardan. He's mine, and he protects me."

"You would be safer with the herd."

"We both know that your king would try to seduce her if he could. We're as one. I'll not let you break that bond. If we can't go together, we don't go at all," I state.

"But you're a vampire. You know this will not come to pass."

I sigh, bow slightly, and place Angelica's hand in the crook of my arm. "So be it. Clearly, your king and the pixies have misjudged me, and I'm not worthy. Thank you for taking the time to talk with us. We'll be on our way."

"Wait!" The fae's face is a mask of confusion. "Let me summon my brother..." he looks at Angelica, "... you met him in the subway on your first night. He'll know what to do."

The fae keeps his back to the wall, maintaining a watchful eye on me. He even walks backward toward the back of the store, making sure I do not attack him.

"What did you do?" asks Angelica.

"It was war. It was also many hundreds of years ago. The fae have long memories but so do the vampires. They killed many of our kind, too."

"How did you survive?"

"That's a complicated story. The easiest answer is, I didn't care if I died. I had already lived a long time by the time the war came to pass. Most of my friends were dead, my children were killed, and I no longer mattered. When it got to the end, I was nothing more than a killing machine. It took a long time for me to accept the fact I was still alive, and all the races had agreed to peace. As the oldest of my kind left, it was assumed I'd take the mantel, but I retreated within myself. I guess you could say I was looking for something, only I didn't know what it was until I met you."

"You had children?"

"Not in the way you're thinking. I have turned three humans into vampires in my very long life. Those are the children I was referring to." A wave of sadness washes over me as I think back to them.

As if she can sense my displeasure, Angelica wraps an arm around my waist and leans against me. "I'm so sorry, Janardan."

"It was a long time ago." I kiss the top of her head and breathe in her scent. "I have you now, and I'm happy. I haven't been that for a very long time."

Angelica pushes up on her tiptoes and kisses me on the cheek. "Ditto."

I grasp her chin and chastely kiss her lips. "You make all those centuries of loneliness worthwhile. You're a blessing, a light at the end of a very dark tunnel."

"A tunnel in which you slaughtered many of our kind," interrupts a voice from the back of the store.

Angelica twists and puts herself between this new fae and me. I go to move in front of her, but she sidesteps so that I can't.

"Angel?" I growl.

Angelica shakes her head and addresses the fae. "How many vampires did you kill? Or does that not matter? Why are the lives of the fae so much more important than theirs? And from what I can gather, all this was a very long time ago. Can't you all just get along?"

The fae approaches us, confusion clouding his features. He is an almost exact clone of the fae who was here before, except his eyes are bright green.

"My brother said the vampire Janardan is here, and that he's blessed and able to walk in the daylight. Is this your doing?"

"I'm Angelica, and this is Janardan. We think I'm the reason he can walk in the sun, but it was a pixie that blessed him, not me." "Liar," hisses the fae.

"And yet you know she's telling the truth. Can you not feel it in your bones? Angelica is the chosen one, and she's mine. We belong to each other, and if the herd does not welcome us, we'll take our leave."

"I'm called Magus, and my brother is Navi. We met the little one when she first transitioned. I fought those demons for you, although they didn't know why they wanted you, only that they did. This compulsion will increase until you come into your powers fully in twenty-eight days. There will be nowhere for you to hide. Someone, whether it be a supernatural or one of your own kind, will try to keep you for themselves. How do you know this vampire isn't trying to keep you for himself?"

"His name is Janardan." Angelica looks over her shoulder at me. "Why do they keep doing that?" I shrug, and she looks back at Magus. "And would he have brought me to you if he were trying to keep me for himself? That doesn't make sense, even to me."

Magus smiles and nods. "True, but vampires can be treacherous."

"So can the fae," I counter.

"Only when we have to. How did it come to pass that a pixie blessed you?"

"It wanted to see my fangs, so I showed him." I glance at Angelica. "Was it a him or a her?"

"He looked like a boy... I mean, male, but..." Angelica shrugs.

"It was indeed a him. And he wanted to see your fangs? Whatever for?"

"I think he was curious. I promised not to hurt him, and he approached. He even tried to touch them." I chuckle. "Then the next thing I know, he's throwing grit in my eyes and disappearing. I wasn't amused, but, of course, I didn't realize he'd blessed me."

Magus stares at me, a small smile on his lips. "You know pixies are closely related to us. Some never become true fae, but we guard them fiercely. That one would approach you and bless *you*, Janardan, is extraordinary."

"I think he liked him," replies Angelica, nodding.

Magus holds out his hand to Angelica. She glances at me, and I nod.

"Take her other hand, vampire, and let's see if the fae will accept you into our realm."

I take Angelica's hand, and like his brother before him, Magus begins to glow and pulsate.

"I do warn you, vampire, if the realm does not accept you, you will feel pain... lots of excruciating pain."

"Hang on a min—" says Angelica as light surrounds us.

For a moment, I do feel pain, but it turns to something else, heat but not unpleasant, and when I open my eyes, we are in a great banquet hall surrounded by the fae.

Angelica looks around, the color has drained from her face, and I catch her as she faints.

"What have you done," I yell at Magus.

"Be calm, Janardan, it can be overwhelming for humans when they come here. They are so young. Your mate will wake up soon. Bring her to the table, the chairs are most comfortable. Here, we'll wait for Oona, Queen of the Fae." "Oona?"

I ask.

Magus nods as he smiles at me knowingly. I have met their queen on the battlefields. I have sunk my teeth into her flesh before her people wrestled her away from me. At the time, she screamed vengeance, but that day vengeance was mine. I slaughtered many and was later told it was because of me that the races found a way to establish peace.

"The fae always have a way to cheat, connive, and deceive, don't you?" I ask bitterly.

"You will not be harmed, Janardan. You have your mate to thank for that. We know that if we hurt you, she'll not look favorably upon us. Our king, Oberon, is eager to meet her. Perhaps she will find him more to her liking, and then our queen may do with you as she wishes."

I cradle Angelica in my arms as I sit at their table. "Not going to happen," I grind out.

"We'll see."

CHAPTER FOURTEEN

Angelica

I feel warm and rejuvenated. When I open my eyes, I am in Janardan's arms at a table surrounded by the fae. They are all very good looking like tall Vikings. Some have dark hair, most have fair hair, and their eyes are all so beautiful. Janardan is talking quietly to someone on his left, and when I stir, all conversations in the hall stop, and he looks down at me and smiles.

"I was beginning to think, angel, that you were not going to wake up. How do you feel?"

I stretch my arms up and yawn. "I feel good. I'm hungry."

Laughter fills the hall, and I look at Janardan, heat filling my cheeks.

"Perhaps you should sit up, and I'll introduce you to everyone?"

"How bad do I look?"

More laughter comes from those around me. Slowly, I sit up at a very long table. There must be thirty fae sitting at it with many more standing behind the chairs.

"How long have I been asleep for?" I ask, twisting to face Janardan.

"About four hours."

The fae sitting next to Janardan chuckles.

"It may only be four hours in human terms, but time works differently here in the realm. You, my dear, have been asleep for far longer than that. That's why you're so hungry."

This man looks different than the others. He's broader across the chest, and his hair is quite dark. It's in braids with little pink flowers all through it, and it should look feminine, but on him, it looks appropriate. His eyes are amber with flecks of gold in them, and from the expression on his face, he's up to no good.

"Are you teasing me?"

"No, not at all." He stands and holds a hand to his chest and bows slightly. "Please, allow me to introduce myself. I'm Oberon, King of the Fae, and your most honorable host."

The king takes my hand and kisses it. He looks me in the eyes before he smiles and lets my hand go. It feels somehow intimate, and I wipe the back of my hand on my jeans.

"Nice to meet you. I'm Angelica Adam, and this is my *mate*, Janardan."

The king roars with laughter. "Indeed. We have already met your *mate*, Angelica, and he's made it clear that you're his."

Janardan rubs my back soothingly.

As I look around the table, it dawns on me that I'm sitting on Janardan's lap. I quickly swivel my head and lock eyes with him.

"What?" he asks.

I lean in and whisper in his ear, "I'm on your lap."

The entire room erupts into laughter. With my face burning, I lean back with eyes wide, staring at Janardan.

He smiles at me. "Supernatural hearing."

"Oh."

I look down at his chest, and he raises my chin, so I have to look at him.

"What is it, Angel?"

"Will I get that?" I whisper.

Janardan shakes his head. "I don't think so. But until you reach your full potential, we won't know." "Hmmm... so not a superhero?"

The room again erupts into laughter, and my face heats up.

"Superhero?" Janardan kisses me lightly. "You will always be that to me."

I glance around, then back at him. "Why?"

"Without you, I wouldn't be able to walk in the sun, and there is no way I'd have been allowed into the troupe and herd's realms. *You* are amazing."

I lean in to kiss him, and it's only when I pull away that I realize the whole room is quiet. I cast a look at Oberon, and he's smiling at me indulgently.

"I truly hope you are the chosen one. For your heart shines so brightly that all can see and feel it." Oberon places both hands over his heart. "You are truly a child of the light."

"Th-thank you?"

Oberon throws his head back in laughter, and the rest of the herd follows suit.

"Oberon, you mentioned before that time works differently here. How long have Angelica and I been here according to human time?"

Oberon smiles, and before he answers, a tall, regal-looking woman with long red hair enters the hall. She appears to glide across the floor, and the fae fall to her feet as she approaches. Oberon stands and drops to one knee, head bowed.

"Oona, my love, it's good to see you," says Oberon.

As I'm sitting on Janardan's lap, I bow my head and hope she doesn't find me rude.

"Oberon, my love, you're always a delight to my eyes."

"And yet, it's been more than a month since I've seen you?"

Oona laughs, and it's a tinkling sound that fills the hall. "And yet, it appears you haven't wasted away without me."

Oberon stands, lips turned down in a grimace that makes his beautiful face appear hard. "I have learned to survive," he replies dryly.

I glance up at the pair of them and find Oona staring at me, disdainfully. I drop my gaze and stare at her feet.

"So, the chosen one has chosen poorly, or at least that's what the court tells me."

I feel my face heat again, but this time in anger as her words sink in. Queen or not, she doesn't get to talk down to Janardan while I'm in the room.

"Oona, I'd be careful if I were you. Her time is nearly upon us, and although I know you don't appreciate Janardan, he is *her mate* and has shown the herd nothing but sincere respect."

"Pfft!" Oona says as she walks away from us. "It wasn't you the vampire nearly killed, my love, *it was me*," Oona screeches at the end.

Janardan moves quickly further away from the fae royals putting me on my feet and behind him.

"It was war, Queen Oona, and you attacked us first. You thought to kill all of us, and may have, if I hadn't gotten the upper hand."

I peek around Janardan, and Oona's face is twisted in rage, turning her beautiful features into something grotesque and unappealing.

"I'll end you," screams Oona.

Oberon moves in front of her. "Be reasonable, my love, we're moments away from—"

Oona pushes him out of the way and begins to chant, holding up her hand, eyes fixed on Janardan. I watch helplessly as he is lifted off the floor and begins to scream, bowed back as though his heart is trying to leave his chest.

"Stop it," I yell, grabbing onto his hand.

Janardan turns his head to look at me. "Run," he painfully screams out.

"I. Will. Not!"

Without too much thought, I go around his prone form and run toward the fae queen. She smiles evilly at me and raises her other hand. I feel a vice around my heart, but it does not slow me down. To everyone's surprise, I reach her, grab her hand, and scream.

"No!"

The very air around her vibrates, and for a moment, her face looks like it does when you are in a wind tunnel, and everything is pulled back. The next thing I know, Queen Oona is flung across the room and slammed against a far wall, fifty feet away. Blood trickles out of the corner of her mouth, and gradually she slides down ending on her ass.

I turn around and run back to Janardan, who is on his knees. "Are you okay?" I ask as I touch his face.

"Yes, my angel, I am." His breathing is ragged, and he looks a little gray around the edges, but he's alive.

Screams erupt around the hall, and I look over my shoulder. A crowd is around the Queen on the floor, and Oberon has tears streaming down his face.

"Shit," I whisper.

Janardan stands, holds out his hand, and guides me to where the Queen is laying. The crowd moves away from us, fear in the eyes of the fae.

"What did you do?" asks Oberon.

"I don't know. I wanted her to stop hurting Janardan. That's all I was thinking of."

Janardan kneels in front of Oona. He reaches for my hand and places the other hand on her chest. The rest of the herd moves in around us, and I'm fearing for my life when Janardan begins to chant. A warm sensation from my chest moves down my arm into Janardan, and slowly, Oona moves. Her body bows, and she lets out a groan, then her eyes shoot open, and she looks startled.

Janardan stops chanting, removes his hand, and moves the both of us back.

Oberon rushes to his wife's side, concern written all over his face. "Oona?"

"Oberon, what happened?"

"It appears, my love, that the vampire saved you."

Shaking her head, Oona allows Oberon to help her to her feet.

"How?" she asks Janardan.

Janardan puts his arm around my waist. "Angelica. Don't ask me the how of it, for I don't know, but I knew if I held onto her and touched you,

I'd be able to fix you."

Oona drops to one knee and whispers, "She is the chosen one."

"So, it would seem," agrees Janardan.

"I thought I had a month to go?"

"Time moves differently here. You're human, in your world, you've been gone for over a month. Time for us is fluid, but as you are of the human race it's different for you," explains Oberon.

"Does this mean I'm older."

Oona stands, shaking her head. "No, Angelica. You're mated to Janardan, so you inherit his immortality. For you, time will cease to matter."

"I'm sorry I hurt you," I whisper, appalled at my actions.

"No, my..." Oona looks at Janardan then Oberon. "What *do* I call her?"

"Angelica is fine," I say.

Shaking her head slightly, Oona continues. "No, it's not. But thank you for letting me use your name. Angelica, it's I who should apologize to you. I let an old wound cloud my judgment, and you were only protecting your mate. I'd have done no less for Oberon."

Oberon's face softens at his queen's admission, and he moves to stand next to her.

"I'm grateful you saved her," states Oberon.

"I'm glad you didn't kill Janardan," I offer her awkwardly.

Queen Oona smiles at me and moves forward, hand extended. As I place my hand in hers, she curtsies.

"Your highness, you're welcome in the realm of the herd, anytime. All you need do is think of us, and we'll come for you. Things are afoot in your realm, and it's time you left and did what you were born to do."

"And what's that?" I ask.

Oona smiles. "Something tells me, you'll figure it out."

"I have a question for you, your highness," says Janardan.

"Speak, Janardan."

"How is it I'm able to feed off Angelica without giving in to the crave?"

Oona smiles. "I believe it's because you're her true mate. You can't exist without her, and she cannot exist without you. You are tied together for eternity."

I look up at Janardan smiling. "Cool!" Janardan smiles at me. "It is indeed, cool." "You need to go," urges Oona.

"How do we—" Light flashes around us, and we find ourselves back in the grocery store with Magus and Navi. "How rude," I mutter.

Magus chuckles while Navi is back in his corner eyeing both of us cautiously.

"Our queen isn't known for long goodbyes." Magus bows to both of us. "May you have many blessings, your highnesses, and may you always be in the light."

"Thank you, Magus. Your queen mentioned there is trouble?" asks Janardan.

Magus straightens. "There is unrest in the city. The supernaturals have turned it upside down searching for Angelica. Subconsciously, the humans know something is wrong, and it makes them nervous. Only you two can repair the city and the peace within it."

"How the hell am I supposed to do that?" I ask.

Navi clears his throat, and we all stare at him.

"One day at a time?"

I grin, and he appears to relax a little.

"That I can do."

"Come on, my angel, let's get you home and feed."

"How did you know I was hungry?"

"You mentioned it before things got pear-shaped in the hall."

"Seems like forever ago."

Right at that, moment my stomach lets out a growl, and I feel heat infuse my cheeks.

Janardan raises my hand to his lips. "Let's go."

It's funny when Janardan said he was taking me home, it didn't occur to me that he'd take me to my old apartment. He didn't, he took me to his place, and as we walked through the door, I felt a sense of comfort wash over me.

Janardan keeps walking into the kitchen, opens the fridge, and frowns.

"That bad?"

"I have a selection of take-out menus. Let me find them."

"I think I'll go shower. Order whatever you'd like."

Janardan immediately stops looking and turns to face me. His eyes are slightly darker, and I suddenly feel like the sexiest woman on earth.

"Want to join me?"

He moves so quickly that I can't track him, and I'm in the bathroom, and he's undressing me before I have had a chance to take a breath.

"Janardan!"

He immediately stops. "What?"

I smile at him, unsure of what I'm upset about and shake my head. "Nothing."

He grins at me, extends one of his fingers into a claw, and kneels in front of me dragging the claw down my jeans, shredding them and my underwear.

"These were my favorites."

He buries his face in my crotch and inhales, his tongue laps at me, and suddenly, I don't care about anything.

I clutch the back of his head, and his laughter reverberates from my pussy to my nipples.
Effortlessly, he lifts and places me on the vanity, all the while his tongue teases me.

"More," I demand, spreading my legs further.

Janardan places two fingers inside of me as he sucks on my clit. The pleasure he's eliciting builds as his tongue laps at me, and he rhythmically moves his fingers in and out.

I'm chasing my release, and it's just there but not quite. "I need more."

Janardan quickly stands and thrusts into me forcefully. I cry out, not in pain but in unexpected pleasure. I tilt my head to the side, offering him my neck. Janardan's fangs extend, and as he pounds into me again, he sinks them deeply into me.

My body reacts immediately as he takes his first pull on my neck by exploding around his cock and milking him for his seed. The orgasm intensifies with each pull on my neck.

"Faster," I scream.

And with the speed that only a supernatural has, he pumps in and out of me all the while drinking from me. My orgasm keeps coming, and I feel him bucking wildly, so I know he's close. Janardan releases my neck and roars as he thrusts in as far as he can go. I look down, and light glows between us, flashing blindly, then dissipates. Unlike last time, we don't pass out.

Janardan picks me up and takes me into his bedroom, keeping us joined. He goes to a chair in the corner of the room and sits down. The chair rocks back, and I can feel he's still hard inside of me. I rock my hips, and he groans. Janardan's hands move to my hips and he begins to move me at a punishing speed. His thumb goes to my clit. I throw my head back in ecstasy as I feel another orgasm building.

"Look at me, angel," says Janardan in a ragged tone.

One look at him, and I can see he's close again.

His fangs are extended, there's blood down his chest, and his eyes are filled with lust as he continues to move my hips.

"Fuck me on the bed."

In a blur, he's moved. I'm on all fours, and he's staring at me in the large mirror that's above his bed.

"Keep your eyes on me," Janardan demands. "Spread your legs further and bow down but keep that head up."

I do as he says, ass in the air, down on my elbows, head up staring at him. Janardan grins then drives into me. The pleasure and pain are so uniquely tied that I can't tell one from the other. He thrusts into me so quickly, and just as I feel myself about to explode, he leans over me and puts his finger on my clit. The ensuing orgasm rips through me, and I scream his name.

But still, his assault on my body continues.

It's as though I was made for him and him me. Like a sword in its scabbard, we fit perfectly. Janardan reaches forward, wrapping my hair around his fist as he bucks wildly three more times. Our eyes are locked on each other in the mirror, and when he reaches his orgasm, I clench my muscles around his cock causing him to grin seductively at me.

A ball of light emerges again hovering above my back, goes into Janardan, then into me. The ball floats out of me, separates into two spheres, one going into each of us.

Janardan disconnects and falls alongside me on the bed. I grin at him as sleep takes over. I feel so relaxed and loved. I feel his hands as he pulls me into him, and he mutters something to me, but I'm too tired to understand what it is.

CHAPTER
FIFTEEN

Angelica

I wake to the smell of bacon, eggs, and coffee. I sit up in bed. Janardan isn't here, so I stand, rifle through his closet, pull out a shirt, and pad into the kitchen in search of the man and the wonderful smell.

Janardan grins at me, pulls me into his side, and kisses me tenderly.

"Did I hurt you?"

I pull back and look at him quizzically. "Only if you call multiple orgasms pain. And if that's the case, honey, you can do that to me anytime."

Blushing, Janardan chuckles and shakes his head. "Hussy."

"Damn straight!"

"Food?"

"Yes, I'm starving."

I pour us both a cup of coffee and take them to the dining table. Janardan joins me with two plates piled high with food.

"Thank you," I whisper as I pick up a piece of bacon and chew.

"You're more than welcome, my angel."

"So, what are we going to do today?"

"We've been summoned to the Council to face all the races."

"Including the humans?"

Janardan shakes his head. "Except for the humans."

"Why no humans?"

"Who's the best one to represent the human race?"

I think about it for a moment and sigh. "That's messy."

"Exactly, so for the moment, only supernaturals."

"And me."

"And you," agrees Janardan.

For a while, I'm happy to eat and enjoy the moment. Before I know it, I've eaten everything on my plate, and I've stolen some bacon off Janardan's plate. He doesn't refuse me, only smiles at me and shakes his head.

"Where did you get the food from?"

"I went back to Magus and Navi to get food, and I stopped by some stores and picked you up some clothes. I hope you don't mind?"

"You bought clothes for me? Where are they?"

"I've washed them. They are hanging in the closet next to the one you stole that shirt out of, and your underwear is in the top drawer of our dresser."

"Our?"

Janardan nods at me solemnly.

"Did I get a whole drawer or just half?"

"A whole drawer."

Not wanting to make him feel weird, I stand and sit on his lap.

"Thank you. Can we get all my stuff and move it in here?"

Janardan nods. "I've already called a moving company, and they are packing up your apartment as we speak."

"What made you think I'd want to move in with you?" I tease.

"The sphere of light. Do you not feel what I feel? It showed me how you felt when you first entered this apartment yesterday. It made me happy."

I grin at him. "You make me happy, too."

A flash of gray runs into the kitchen, and I jump off Janardan's lap and run after it. My beautiful cat, Grace, is sitting in front of empty dishes meowing up at me.

"Grace!" I bend and pick her up. "Oh, my baby, I'm a bad momma. I forgot about you."

Janardan chuckles and walks toward us, ruffling Grace's fur.

"She eats an awful lot."

"Grace is a piggy, and you can't keep feeding her 'cause she doesn't know when to stop," I say as I kiss the top of her head.

"Hmmm... I've opened two cans of food for her already."

Laughter bubbles up out of me. "She'll tell you I don't feed her, but she lies."

I put her on the ground and kiss Janardan's face.

"She makes you happy?"

"Yes, but so do you, and thank you for getting her."

He smiles and kisses my nose. "The movers rang and said they'd found her. Grace scratched the hell out of me on the way back. She's stronger than she looks."

"Did you run back here?"

"Yes."

"Well, no wonder. It scares me half to death, imagine how she feels."

Janardan nods seemingly unconvinced as he looks down at the furball who's licking the bottom of her empty food dish.

"Did I mention I bought you clothes?" "Yes," I squeal.

I run into his bedroom and fling open the closet. There are three pairs of jeans, just like the ones he ripped off me, T-shirts, shirts, and all of them are exactly my style. Next, I go to the dresser and open it. The underwear is all a little risqué for me, and I frown.

"Don't frown, the underwear is for me."

"But it's not comfortable for everyday wear."

"Look in the top right-hand corner."

I move the plethora of colors and styles aside and find three pairs of black cotton panties. I grin at him, and he shakes his head.

"I prefer the lacy ones."

"And I'll keep that in mind, but it's nice to wear comfies every now and again."

"Indeed."

I run to him and throw my arms around his neck.

"When do we have to be at the Council meeting?"

Janardan holds up his wrist and looks at his watch. "In one and a half hours."

I let him go and screech, "What?"

"What is it, my angel?"

I shake my head from side to side. "You should have woken me earlier. It's going to take me an hour to get ready."

"You have time."

"Makeup? Did you buy makeup?" I ask, verging on panic.

"No, you don't need it."

"Of course, I need it. Can you go get me some?"

"Angelica, you don't—"

"Look inside you, Janardan. Do you *not* feel my panic?"

He frowns at me and looks down. "Fine, get in the shower. I'll be as fast as I can." In a blur, he leaves me alone.

I stride into the bathroom and take a warm shower. By the time I've washed my hair and body and towel-dried everything, Janardan has returned with three shopping bags full of cosmetics, cleansers, and creams.

"Thank you, I love you," I whisper as I check out all the pretties.

"You do mean me, right?"

I swivel my head to him and kiss his cheek. "Of course. You can pick my underwear if you like?"

This seems to please him, and he saunters out of the bathroom.

Fifty minutes later, I come out, hair and makeup done looking for clothes. Laying on the bed is a red lace bra and panties, a pair of blue jeans and a black shirt. When I put the ensemble on, I'm impressed at how the black shirt hugs my figure accentuating my bust line. Looking down at my feet, I walk into the living room. Janardan is staring out at the street, a pair of black three-quarter inch heels dangling off his fingertip.

"Yay!" I run over and take them from him.

Janardan arches an eyebrow and takes them back then I pout at him.

He shakes his head. "Sit."

I sit on his brown leather armchair, and he kneels in front of me, placing the strappy shoes on my feet. "Tonight, I need you to stay close to me. I feel as though your powers are amplified when we're together, touching."

"That makes sense. The books that Aran went through said that we're stronger together."

Janardan nods as he does up one shoe then goes

to work on the other. "Please, don't put yourself into any danger. Stay close," repeats Janardan.

"I will."

"Angelica?" he says sternly.

"What? I will!"

"You better." Janardan leans in and kisses me softly, sniffing me as he does. "Your scent has changed. It's heavenly. You ready?" Blushing, I reply, "Let's do this."

As we walk into the Council chambers, you can feel the magic in the air. All the different races are there, all in their true forms. For me, the demons are the hardest to look at. Janardan squeezes my hand slightly, and I stare up at him.

"I'm with you."

I smile at him, and he guides me to a seat at a large round table. Not knowing what to do, I sit down, and then so do all the other races.

"Do you feel it?" asks a demon.

Most around the table nod.

I look at each face in turn, amazed at how quickly my life has changed in a matter of days. I had no idea that all these creatures were real, and now here I am sitting at their Council table as they look at me expectantly. I stand, and so does everyone else.

"Ah, no, please sit." Everyone re-takes their seats. "I'm not sure how this is supposed to work. It's not like I've done this before."

A male vampire stands, glaring at me. "She's mated to a vampire, so she's ours to protect." "No!" yells the demon.

And then all hell breaks loose. People are shouting and snarling at each other. I look down at Janardan, and he takes my hand.

In a small voice, I whisper, "Please stop."

Immediately, the room goes quiet. The vampire goes to speak, and I hold up a finger. He stops, shakes his head, and tries to speak again, but nothing comes out.

"Cool," I say, grinning. "I think the first order of business is to decide how to bring the humans into the Council. I'd appreciate all of your assistance in deciding how best to do this."

Everyone except the vampire begins to talk at once.

"One at a time," I say. I point at the demon. "You may go first."

He stands, smiling at me broadly. Holding a hand

to his chest, he bows slightly and says, "Baracus, your highness."

"Hello, Baracus, I'm Angelica."

"Oh, I know."

Most around the table chuckle, and it breaks the ice, so to speak. The rest of the night goes well. I feel like I've accomplished something. The races all appear to be getting along. I solved a dispute between the vampires and the fae, and the whole time Janardan was there to support and encourage me. At the end of the night, I felt like I was born to do this.

That is until it came time to farewell the delegates.

The vampire who I later came to know as Leviathan, bows to show his respect and reverence to me. He takes my hand and inhales, his fangs extend, and he smiles creepily at me then winks at Janardan.

"For she'll come into her power in her twentyfifth year, and when she touches the dutiful, their true selves will become known her. She will be allpowerful and guide us to redemption with her true mate and protector at her side. All will fear them for they shall rule the races. Their offspring will lead us into the new millennium and bring about a ruling race."

"What the hell does that mean?" asks Hunter, alpha to the lycans.

"It means, dog, she's pregnant to a vampire. So who do you think the ruling race will be?" taunts Leviathan.

Janardan pales and pulls me to him breathing deeply. He cups my face with his hands. "It's why your scent changed."

"What?" I loud whisper.

"Is it true?" asks Hunter.

I shake my head at Janardan. "I didn't think it possible, my angel. To my knowledge, no vampire has ever reproduced."

"So, it's true?" demands Hunter.

I look out over the crowd, and I can feel their distrust and anger begin to build.

"We don't know what it means. It could mean the humans will be the ruling race."

"What," yells one of the elvin delegates.

"Or not," I whisper.

Janardan wraps his arm around my waist, and he carries me out of the room and away from the angry mob as fast as his legs will carry him. At one point, I look down, and we are above water. Cringing, I hold on tighter to him, and he chuckles.

"I'll not drop you. The water will help dissipate our scent. When we hit the coast of England, I will stop."

"What? England? As in the UK?"

"You're going to love it."

"Janardan?"

"It's all I could think of to keep you and our child safe."

"We need to work on your communication skills," I grumble. "And don't you get tired?"

"No, I don't. It won't take long, and we'll be there."

"Then what?" I ask down heartedly. "Oh! And what about Grace?"

"I'll send for her. There are those on the Council who are loyal to you. While you spoke, I watched. More than one of them are on your side and will do as you ask."

"But not the vampires?"

Janardan kisses me passionately. "Whatever happens, we'll face this together."

"Okay," I sigh. "I'm hungry."

"Why am I not surprised?"

"I'm eating for two."

"How do you know it's only two?"

"What?" I screech.

Janardan chuckles, kisses my temple, and keeps running.

I know in my heart whatever happens, so long as we face this together, we'll be a force to be reckoned with.

THE END

Continues in
Mazarine – The Affinity Chronicles Book Two
Coming Soon
If you liked this story, you might also like:

The Savage Angels MC Series by
Kathleen Kelly

Savage Stalker Book 1

BLURB

Isn't it funny?

Cardinal

How one accident can change your entire path.

I was an international rock star and the female lead singer for the Grinders, but now I'm hiding in the mountains away from everything and everyone.

That is until the President of the Savage Angels MC, Dane Reynolds gave me a reason to feel again.

He's fierce, strong and loyal, but someone sinister hides in the shadows.

Can Dane save Kat? Or will the savage stalker get to her first?

Savage Fire Book 2

Savage Town Book 3

Savage Lover Book 4

Savage Sacrifice Book 5

Savage Rebel (Novella) Book 6

Savage Lies Book 7

Savage Life Book 8

Savage Christmas (Novella) Book 9

Savage Angels MC Collection Books 1 – 3 Savage Angels MC Collection Books 4 – 6

Kathleen Kelly

The Grinders Series

Truth Book One

Other Books

Crude Possession (Standalone)
Snake's Revenge (Novella)
Spark – The MacKenny Brothers Book 1

ACKNOWLEDGMENTS

Thank you dear reader for reading this tale. I hope you enjoyed reading it as much as I enjoyed writing it.

Part two will be out a little later in 2020.

If you'd like to show me your support, I'd appreciate it if you left me a review on Amazon, Goodreads or BookBub.

Cardinal

If you're feeling particularly generous, all three.

Check these links for more books from
Author K. Kelly

READER GROUP

Want access to fun, prizes and sneak peeks?
Join my Facebook Reader Group.
https://bit.ly/32X17pv

NEWSLETTER

Want to see what's next?
Sign up for my Newsletter.
https://www.subscribepage.com/kathleenkellyauthor

GOODREADS

Add my books to your TBR list on
my Goodreads profile.
http://bit.ly/1xsOGxk

AMAZON

Buy my books from my Amazon profile.
https://amzn.to/2JCUT6q

WEBSITE

https://kathleenkellyauthor.com/

TWITTER

https://twitter.com/kkellyauthor

INSTAGRAM

https://instagram.com/kathleenkellyauthor

EMAIL

kathleenkellyauthor@gmail.com

FACEBOOK

https://bit.ly/36jlaQV

ABOUT THE AUTHOR

K. Kelly was born in Penrith, NSW, Australia. When she was four, her family moved to Brisbane, QLD, Australia. Although born in NSW she considers herself a QUEENSLANDER!

She married her childhood sweetheart, and they live in Toowoomba with their fur baby.

She enjoys writing contemporary, romance novels with a little bit of erotica. She draws her inspiration from family, friends, and the people around her. She can often be found in cafes writing and observing the locals.

If you have any questions about her novels or would like to ask her a question, she can be contacted via email: kathleenkellyauthor@gmail.com or she can be found on Facebook. She loves to be contacted by those who love her books.